Moan in my Mouth

Xtasy

Lock Down Publications and Ca$h Presents
Moan in my Mouth
A Novel by *Xtasy*

Moan in my Mouth

Lock Down Publications
Po Box 944
Stockbridge, Ga 30281

Visit our website @
www.lockdownpublications.com

Copyright 2022 by Xtasy
Moan in my Mouth

All rights reserved. No part of this book may be reproduced in any form or by electronic or mechanical means, including information storage and retrieval systems without permission in writing from the publisher, except by a reviewer who may quote brief passages in review.
First Edition July 2022
Printed in the United States of America

This is a work of fiction. Names, characters, places, and incidents either are products of the author's imagination or are used fictitiously. Any similarity to actual events or locales or persons, living or dead, is entirely coincidental.

Lock Down Publications
Like our page on Facebook: Lock Down Publications @
www.facebook.com/lockdownpublications.ldp
Book interior design by: **Shawn Walker**
Edited by: **Jill Alicea**

Stay Connected with Us!

Text **LOCKDOWN** to 22828 to stay up-to-date with new releases, sneak peaks, contests and more…
Thank you.

Moan in my Mouth

Submission Guideline.

Submit the first three chapters of your completed manuscript to ldpsubmissions@gmail.com, subject line: Your book's title. The manuscript must be in a .doc file and sent as an attachment. Document should be in Times New Roman, double spaced and in size 12 font. Also, provide your synopsis and full contact information. If sending multiple submissions, they must each be in a separate email.

Have a story but no way to send it electronically? You can still submit to LDP/Ca$h Presents. Send in the first three chapters, written or typed, of your completed manuscript to:

**LDP: Submissions Dept
Po Box 944
Stockbridge, Ga 30281**

DO NOT send original manuscript. Must be a duplicate.

Provide your synopsis and a cover letter containing your full contact information.

Thanks for considering LDP and Ca$h Presents.

Xtasy

Chapter 1
-Cupid-

Life is simple for a man like me. I can honestly say that I never lacked anything. I practically had everything handed to me. The only child of a very wealthy mother and father. I received my doctorate in science and my masters in human behavior.

My father, Elvin, wanted me to follow in his footsteps to carry on the family legacy of gold trading, but I had plans of my own. Since a kid, I've always found adventure in getting into trouble. I was a mischievous teen who got a thrill off of girls. I had a thing for knocking the next guy for his girl. At times, it turned out to be a dangerous game, but I had a thing for laughing danger right in the face. Two things I found comfort in; money and women. I could never get enough of the two.

The truth is that money is the root of all evil. I don't doubt that one bit. But, I know for a fact, that pussy is neck and neck with money. The two greatest things God created for mankind.

God gave us all talents, and He desires for us to use them. No matter what the talents are. It could be the gift of gab, or even hustling or my favorite. Making a woman cum! God gave me two of the greatest gifts a man could have. One, I'm a master at making a woman cum. Secondly, I can make money with my eyes closed. I do it every day.

God really blessed me. He made my tongue longer than the norm and wider than the average. My saliva glands are supreme. My tongue stays wet. My dick, who I nicknamed, OG, which is short for Oh God because that's the first thing women say when I pull him out is exceptional and good at what he does.

OG is nine and a half inches long. Facts, I measured him. And he's as wide as my wrist. He's got two long, thick veins that run down both sides. The head of OG is plump and soft, like a Georgia peach. Women love when I play with their clitoris with the head of OG. OG has gotten me into a lot of trouble. Once a woman gets a taste of him, she's hooked. It's like a syringe of the

Xtasy

best china white money could buy. The only difference is, once you're hooked on OG, there is no rehab, you're hooked for life.

Women take one look at me, I'm a hundred and seventy pounds, six feet, with smooth dark skin and wavy hair. My body is chiseled tight. My shoulders are leg rest for women. I often applaud myself on how tight my six-pack is. I have to give all the credit to my sex game. My hip thrust is the ultimate six-pack workout.

Women, they get me, always telling me that I'm the man for them, the man of their dreams. I tell them, "only if it was a wet dream" I can never, ever, ever! Be a one-woman man. Tying me down isn't a part of God's plans. But, I can tell you what is. He wants me to become a self-made millionaire and my favorite; make as many women as I possibly can, cum!

***

"Uhmm, babe. Where are you going?" My Thursday night special asked me as I sat up in bed.

I covered OG with the sheet to keep him warm. I protected him with my life. I could never let a woman say OG didn't turn out when he was called upon to perform.

"I have to go, baby doll," I said, calling her what I called every woman when I couldn't remember their name. "I don't want to be late for work," I said as I looked at her half-naked body. The sheet covered her ass as her plump titties pointed at me like a snitch on the witness stand.

"You can never be late, you're the boss, or did you forget you own the place!" she laughed.

I saw where this was going. That was why I never fucked a woman at her house, then stay the night. It seemed like every time I did, the woman would try to keep me; like I was a stray dog.

Irritated, I stood up, grabbed my jeans, and stepped into them. I never wore briefs, well not when I wore jeans. OG sweated really hard when I wore briefs with jeans. Like I said before, I protected him with my life.

Moan in my Mouth

As I buckled my Gucci belt, babydoll eyed my six-pack. I looked around the floor for my shirt. I couldn't remember where I'd tossed it. Last night, as soon as we hit the room, clothes got tossed, then I tossed her.

"Looking for this?" Babydoll asked, turning my attention to her. She was naked; like she'd just entered the world. Her backside was facing me, her legs wide apart as she bent over with her head between her legs. She stared at me, her Garden of Eden on full display.

I walked up behind her with the intention to get my shirt. She held her acrobatic position as I walked up. I really didn't try hard, because I was addicted. Pussy was my poison. Grabbing her by her hips, I grinded OG all over her backside. "Uhm!" she moaned as I continued to grind into her.

I moved my hand to her warmth, my fingers grazed her sex lips. She gasped as I tightened my grip on her hips. "Can you at least stay for ten more minutes?" She begged.

I laughed. "You know, like I know ten minutes is not enough time. I need at least ten minutes of foreplay to get going." I said as I let her hips go. I stood still, she grinded into my midsection like we were at the club.

"We have time," she said. "Can I just pay you to stay awhile?"

This wouldn't be the first time a woman has begged me to stay or the first time one has offered me money to have sex with them. I honestly didn't find it interesting to have sex with the same woman, back-to-back. Once OG felt the inside of a woman's walls, he first has to unfamiliarize himself with her in order to fuck her again.

"I tell you what," I said. She stood up with a big smile on her face. I unbuckled my belt buckle. Her eyes followed my hands like a crazed stalker as my jeans fell to the floor. OG was freed yet again. I stroked OG as he rose like the sun.

"I want you to get OG down your throat, all the way down to his twin brothers. If you can't, then I'm leaving, and we'll try again in a month."

Xtasy

It looked as if OG was staring at her to see if she was up to the challenge. No woman had ever had him fully down her throat. Many have tried, but none has ever accomplished the task.

Babydoll stared at OG with one eyebrow raised. She stepped toward me slowly. She wanted another round of OG, but she knew getting him to fit inside her small mouth would be like having a baby from her mouth. Her jaws would be stretched to capacity. - their limit

I pretended to pull my jeans back up. "Should I?" I asked as my jeans came above my knees.

She held her hand up as she kneeled down in front of me. OG flexed for her like a baby's arm on steroids. Babydoll licked her lips. She hesitated as she formed her mouth around OG. The tip of her tongue set him off. Her mouth was tight like a virgin. She had spit bubbles on her tongue that was warm, and wet like a bubble bath. Babydoll laid her tongue flat so that she could take more of him in.

"Work them jaws, Babydoll." I encouraged her. I've waited a long time for a woman to take OG all the way down her throat. I can't lie, I was excited. And as hard as OG was, I knew he was excited too. We both were hoping she could finally be the one.

Babydoll worked her jawbone muscles at the same time she worked her hand around the base of OG. She moaned and bobbed her head up and down like she knew what she was doing. On the cool, she didn't.

"Wet him up some more," I gave her some pointers. "Move your teeth back," I said as I felt her gnawing at OG.

Just like women had certain desires for how they wanted their pussy eaten, men had specific desires for how we wanted our dick sucked. Women always thought that just popping the dick in their mouth, and bobbing their head up and down was all there was to it. Not for OG. OG had many different ways he liked to be sucked. He was like an ocean. Once you crossed over him, he wouldn't be the same ocean as before. What OG liked the first time, sometimes didn't work the next time.

Moan in my Mouth

OG likes to be wet up first. Nobody enjoys a dry rubdown. An oily massage was the best massage. OG hated to be squeezed. Grip him, but never squeeze him. He couldn't cum if he couldn't breathe. And one thing he hated was teeth. Babydoll did as instructed as she eased her teeth back. She worked her wet tongue around him. She wet OG up just the way he liked it. He started to grow right before her eyes. He tried his best to slide down her throat. Her tonsils blocked her hole like a lineman blocking for Tom Brady.

Babydoll adjusted herself on her knees as she looked up at me with OG dangling from her wet mouth. She sucked and slurped as OG inched his way down her throat farther and farther. Babydoll moaned, but it sounded more like a gargle. She did her best to make her cheeks adjust to his size. I rocked my hips forward as the pleasure took me to another dimension. OG was halfway in, and halfway out, just dying to touch the bottom of her throat.

Babydoll's eyes watered as her gagging sounds turned into choking sounds. I slowed my hips down to give her a chance to catch her breath. She looked like she was determined to be the first woman to swallow OG whole. Babydoll gripped my ass and pulled me in deeper down her throat. I felt the flood gate open before she noticed what was happening.

"Ughhh!" Babydoll vomited all over OG. I jumped back to try to avoid the assault of her vomit pouring from her mouth. Babydoll covered her mouth and looked away embarrassed. It wasn't the first time it's happened to me, and it probably won't be the last.

"Oh my god, I'm so sorry. I swear -" She said, wiping her mouth with the back of her hand.

I snatched the bed sheet up and cleaned OG off. My facial expression looked like I was disgusted, but on the inside, I felt a sense of pride, oh God won again!

Babydoll ran to the bathroom and slammed the door behind herself. I'd witnessed that numerous times too. She'll stay inside the bathroom until she gets the courage to unlock the door. When she finally does decide to come out, I'll be long gone. But there

Xtasy

will be a note on her bed explaining how it's okay, and that I had to go to work. She'll give herself a few days, and then she'll text me. I'll read it, but I won't respond. I'll be too busy knee-deep in another woman's paradise!

$$$

Chapter 2
-Cupid-

Fridays happen to be my favorite day of the week. Friday just seems like the day of relief. I know the bible says God died on a Friday, I wouldn't doubt it one bit. If I could choose a day to die, it'll be Friday too. It was something about Friday. The last day of the workweek. For some, it's payday. For party animals, it's the day to turn up.

Fridays were my day to unwind. Get a clean shave, and a haircut, and pick up my clothes from the dry cleaners. Friday nights, I would usually attend a club or some type of get-together. But not this Friday. This Friday would be a little different.

Today, my best friend from grade school was moving back to Dallas with his new fiance. Cedrick and I had gone to school together all the way from Elementary to High School. After graduating high school, I went to college at the University of Knoxville, and Cedrick went to college in California at UCLA.

When Cedrick called and told me that he was moving back home, I was excited. When he moved away, we rarely saw each other, but we kept in contact. I had missed my bro! We had grown up together tossing chicks. We used to compete to see how many chicks we could flip a week. Majority of the time, I would win, but Cedrick wasn't no slouch. I was surprised when Cedrick told me that he was engaged. Even more shocked when he said she was moving to Dallas with him. I had never seen her, not even a picture.

I parked outside of Cedrick's new house. He actually picked a nice area to buy a home in. Collin County was a nice high-class neighborhood. Good school district if you had kids. The area was well put together. Cedrick could definitely afford it, being that he was the head A & R at Bloody Lyrics records. I had to give it to him; my guy had an ear for talent.

Back in high school, Cedrick used to host talent shows for the school and pay the winner out of his pocket. He was just that much into music. Cedrick and I had a lot in common. He had an ear for

13

music, and I had a mind to create movies. Cedrick needed a beat and a soundboard. Me, I needed a camera and moans.

Cedrick's candy red 2013 Mercedes Benz G63 pulled up, along with a silver and black 2018 Porsche 911. A large U-Haul pulled up and parked behind the Porsche. Cedrick stepped out of his truck with a pair of Tom Ford frames on. His frames matched his tan linen fit.

Cedrick smiled as I walked up to him. "Looking good, Cupid!" We embraced as we shared a laugh.

"Did you expect anything less?" I asked, laughing.

"Never!" he smiled. "The city still looks the same from when we were kids."

I nodded as I shielded my forehead with my hand to block the hot rays of the sun. "I know," I said. "The only part of Dallas that keeps improving is the nice areas. Don't go to Oakcliff or West Dallas. It looks worse than it did back then."

"What about the South?" He asked.

I looked at him like he knew better than to ask something like that. "Don't get me started on South Dallas." We both laughed.

I felt sorry for South Dallas. Don't get me wrong, the unity the south had was amazing, but the only unification they had was going violent. Someone once told me, "If you want to find the hood in every city, look for Martin Luther King Blvd." Why that was, I wouldn't be able to tell you the real truth behind it. But if you ask me, my perspective is, it was to spit on Martin Luther's name.

"Does pawpaw still set the streets on fire with his turkey legs?"

I nodded as I practically tasted my grandfather's famous turkey legs. He was so known for his turkey legs that his friends gave him the nickname, Turkey Leg. My mother calls him Turkey Baby. His turkey legs were so good, that once you pick the bone up, all the meat falls from the bone. He had a saying, "if there's a piece of meat on the bone, the turkey leg is free." The last time he gave a turkey leg away, I was in middle school.

Moan in my Mouth

"He hasn't been on the grill since the pandemic. But thankfully, he's still working his first love."
" Nawl, he's still building houses?" Cedrick asked, shocked.
"Who's going to stop him. The man is a dog past old as hell, and he still wakes up at five-thirty every morning, happily, to go climb a ladder.
"I hope I'm like that when I get his age," Ced said.
I smirked at him. "You work in the A/C with billion-dollar business owners, stop it." We shared a laugh.
"So, where's this fiance of yours?" I asked as I looked at the Porsche.
"She's in the car, acting shy," he waved at the Porsche.
"Amy, you can't hide in the car forever, you do live here now," he laughed.
"Amy?" I looked at him. "Wow, an African American woman named Amy. That's a first."
He smiled. "Who said she was African American."
The door to the Porsche opened. Amy stepped out with a pair of Gucci sunglasses on. I don't know if it was the rays from the sun, or God telling me something. But Amy looked like she had floated from a cloud, right in front of me. I was praying that Cedrick wasn't looking at me look at his fiance, 'cause if he did, he would see the drool coming from the corner of my mouth.
"Beautiful, isn't she?" Ced asked.
"Huh!" I managed to say. Amy walked up to me with a pink pair of soccer shorts on and a matching Polo v-neck. Her long dirty blonde hair was wrapped around into a tight bun of a ponytail.
"Baby, this is my best friend, and my best man, Cupid." I looked at Cedrick as he called me his best man. I wondered if he would've still called me his best man if he found out the thoughts I visioned of his fiance.
"Best man," I wasn't shocked as I made it seem, but I was taken aback.

"Who better?" he smiled. He had a point. We had two other close friends from high school we kept in contact with, but neither was better than me.

"You got a point," I said as I looked at Amy from the corner of my eye. I was afraid to look at her in the eyes, I didn't want to be rude, or should I say perverted, and stare.

"I've heard so much about you, Cupid," She extended her hand. "Ced talks about you all the time." Her hand was soft, and small in my fairly large hand. She looked at me, but behind her shades, I couldn't tell where her eyes were.

"All good things, I hope." I looked at Cedrick as I forced myself to let Amy's hand go.

"Sometimes," she smiled. I looked at their new home, her smile was just too much.

"Are y'all going to move in, or are we going to bake in this hot sun all day?" I joked.

"Well men, it's on ya'll. I'll direct the movers," Amy said.

I nodded. I didn't mind a woman taking charge every now and then. Amy walked in front of us as the movers stepped out of the U-Haul. As Amy walked in front of me, I shook my head. An Asian with a fat ass. What was the world coming to?

"Cupid, it's going to be like old times," Cedrick gripped my shoulder. "It's good to be back."

***

-Cedrick-

"Wow!" Cupid sighed as he wiped the sweat from his forehead. We had just finished moving the last pieces of furniture inside the house. I sat on the couch. Amy pinched my shoulder. "Ouch!"

"No, you not sitting on my favorite couch sweating the way you are. Get up!" She said, I shook my head. Women were weird. They had a favorite lamp, favorite curtain, and a favorite couch.

Moan in my Mouth

Amy only sat on her favorite couch when she was entertaining a company.

"You got it, love," I said as I stood up. I kissed her and pulled her close to me, hugging her sweaty and all.

"Ugh! Get off!" she laughed as she playfully punched me. Cupid stood to the side as he laughed at us.

"Come on Q," I called Cupid the nickname we gave him in middle school. "Let's start putting together the man cave." I led the way to the basement. When Amy and I were looking for a new house, I told her that I had to have a man cave. I felt like every man deserved to have one. I mean, women decorated the entire house. The living room, dining room, kitchen, bathroom, and especially the bedrooms. Men should at least get one room, and what room is better than the man cave.

My man cave was going to be different from most. For one, being an A&R director, I needed a small recording studio. That was mandatory. I also needed a bar and a fridge to hold all of my vintage wine and liquor. A pool table, and a poker table for when I held fella's night. And a projector for when I watched the game and big fights. Let's not forget, my favorite chair. The most comfortable chair known to man. The lazy boy.

Cupid picked up an old picture of us that was stuffed inside one of the boxes. It was of our first day of high school.

"So, what do you think?" I asked as I grabbed two cold Bud Lights from the fridge. I handed one to him.

"It's a great house," he said as he placed the picture back in the box. "Can't believe you still have this," he added.

I laughed. "I wasn't talking about the house. I was talking about Amy.

"Oh, she's nice. I mean from what I've seen, she's a helluva catch. Different from what you used to date, but she's beautiful."

I smiled. His approval meant a lot. He was my best friend. I knew if he felt something was wrong with her, he would've told me. At least I hoped he would've.

Xtasy

Cupid grabbed two pool sticks and passed me one. "Being that you're my best man, are you ready?" He lined up the balls as he placed the triangle over them.

"Of course! Why wouldn't I be? Have you two set a date yet?"

"Not yet. But she wants to either get married in the springtime or the winter. I tried to tell her to let's go ahead and do it now, but she's like, it's too hot." We laughed.

"She's got a point. Black people in tuxedos in a hundred and ten-degree weather scream sweaty pictures." He laughed.

I shook my head and laughed. "So, what about me?"

"When do you plan on settling down and getting married?"

He laughed like he was at a Kevin Hart stand-up." Me, settling down, never! I'ma bachelor for life!"

$$$

Chapter 3
-Cupid-

"Morning, Mr. Patterson!" My head security guard Chad greeted me as I walked into the building.

"Chad, you've been working for me for two years now. I'ma tell you today like I've told you the first day when I hired you, call me, Cupid. My father is, Mr. Patterson."

"I apologize, Cupid. I was just raised to call people by their last name in the business world."

"This isn't a business, Chad. This is family. Do you call your family by their last names?"

Chad laughed. "No sir."

"Sir, is also for my father," I smiled.

"You got it, Cupid."

I dap'd him up and headed towards my office. I was the owner -. No, let me rephrase that. I am the proud owner of the number one exotic film industry on the east coast, Pandora's Poison.

Pandora's Poison wasn't just like most porn industries; we didn't just make ten-minute porn clips to place all over the internet for free. Nah, we were a professional award-winning film industry. The films we made would put Fifty Shades to shame.

When I tell people what I did for a living, they mostly laugh. I get two different reactions all the time. Women often look at me like I'm a creep. Men, on the other hand, always applaud me when I tell them what I do for a living. They would always ask me how many of the women I slept with. I always broke their heart when I tell them, "none."

Like I said before, I was a professional. As well as the rest of my team. Each actor had to go through numerous screening tests. A full physical was done by our in-house physicians. That included STD checks and weekly Aids tests which were made public to the entire staff. We kept a very safe work environment. I was so professional, rain, sleet, or snow, or even a hundred-degree weather, I wore a suit to work. All of the men were ordered to wear casual wear, as well as the women.

Xtasy

My building was located in Frisco, Texas. It was a three-story building that cost me an arm and a leg when I first bought it in 2018. Over the past three years, it seems to have paid for itself. The place is lavish. I made sure to have custom-made everything. I wanted actors to walk inside my place of business and say, "This is where I want to work." I wanted them to all feel like this is home.

"Hey, good morning Cupid!" My secretary Karen greeted me as I walked to her desk, which was directly outside my office.

Karen was twenty-five years old. She was a beautiful Hispanic woman with a vanilla skin complexion. She had long hair that hung down to her shoulders. A slim waist with fairly large titties. She didn't have much ass, but it had a nice curve to it.

Karen and I never had sex, but on several occasions, she's made attempts at, OG. Don't get me wrong, if she didn't work for me, I would've spanked her pussy and made her fix me some lemon-lime fajitas as soon as we were finished. I had a strict rule, never mix business with pleasure. It got hard at times, but it was for the best.

"Morning, Karen," I greeted her back. "Nice hair color, it suits you."

Karen smiled. "Thanks! Nice of you to notice." She stood up and opened my office door for me. I walked into my office and took my suit jacket off. I hung it on my coat rack and walked to my desk.

"Is Camilla here yet?" I asked of my best actor who was due to film a new movie I wrote called, Drink from my river.

"She's upstairs right now. She got here a little before you did."

"Good! Have them set the studio up, we'll start filming in thirty minutes," I scooted my chair out and sat down. I looked up at Karen, she had an unsure look on her face. "You okay, Karen?"

Karen played with her hands nervously. "I have something I want to discuss with you."

Moan in my Mouth

"Ain't nobody harassing you here, are they?" I asked concerned with the whole #metoo movement going on, I made sure to be very careful of all women that worked for me.

"No, it's not that. Everyone here is wonderful. It's just-" She stopped hesitantly as she tried to gain the courage to say what was on her mind.

"Karen, you know you can tell me anything," I assured her.

"I know," she said then sighed. "I'm putting my two weeks' notice in today." She finally said.

She caught me by surprise. I definitely didn't expect her to say that. "Huh?" I asked curiously.

"It's not you or anyone here. I just thought I should go back to school. My daughter Maria had a bring your mom to work day at school the other day. I felt bad that I lied to all the kids there. I didn't know how to tell them I worked at a porn industry."

I raised my finger up. "Not just any porn industry. The best, porn industry." I smiled.

Karen laughed and said. " I love working here. I love working for you, Cupid. But, I thought if any time was good enough to go back to school, would be now. Maria's in school, I have enough money saved up, I'm still young."

I nodded. I understood where she was coming from. Being a single parent had been hard on her in the beginning. But she kept her head on straight and fought through it. I was actually proud of the woman she had become.

"I'm proud of you for wanting to go back to school to climb the ladder of success. If there is anything you'll ever need, I'm always here for you. And if you ever decide to come back, the door will always be open for you."

I stood up and hugged her. "Thank you, Cupid!"

***

Ding!

The elevator opened as it stopped on the third floor. My Stacy Adams sounded off the marble floor as I walked through the hall.

The third floor was used for filming. I had three studios on the third floor, two were in use by my junior producers.

I walked into the third studio, people were moving about getting everything set up for the final scene. Camilla sat in a high chair as a makeup artist did her makeup. She scrolled through her phone as they pampered her to perfection.

Camilla reminded me of Jamila Velazques that played on the hit TV show, Empire. Camilla was one of my favorite actors. She was easy to work with, and she understood my goal. I worked with a few other actors, who were just plain ol' porn stars. Camilla, when she stood in front of a camera, it was like she made love to the camera, instead of her partner.

"Camilla, darling!" I kissed her on the cheek.

"Cupid! Hey handsome!" She greeted me.

"I see you're getting pampered up. You just about ready?" She nodded as she took her gum out of her mouth and placed it on a piece of paper.

"I'm ready when you are," she smiled.

"Okay. You can meet me by prop two while I go check on Roman." She stood up and took her robe off. Under her robe, she wore a tight black Dior dress. Black was her signature color.

I walked over to Roman, who was one of my top male actors. Roman was black and Puerto Rican. He had a long ponytail that he kept in a hair wrap. His skin was golden. He stood at six feet, weighing a hundred and eighty-five pounds. Like me, he was a workout freak. Roman had tried his hand at acting in movies years back but never receive any major roles. He almost gave up on his dream, until I reached out to him two years ago to star in my debut movie, "Cumming From Where I'm From." Cumming From Where I'm From turned out to be a hit, and it put Roman on the mainstream like he always wanted.

"My main man, Roman!" I slapped fives with him.

"Cupid, you ready to make another hit?" Roman asked, displaying his sparkly white teeth.

"Like DJ Khaled say,"

"Another one." Roman finished my sentence.

Moan in my Mouth

"Camilla's ready when you are."
He nodded. "Let's do this. " he sounded excited. What man wouldn't be when he was about to make love with a very beautiful Latina woman, free of charge, plus he gets paid to do it.

I clapped my hands to get everyone's attention. "Everyone! I want to thank you for being here today. Before we make another hit, I want you all to know, I'll never trade you all for the world."

Everyone clapped as some whistled. Camilla patted me on the ass as she walked by looking like a goddess in her tight black dress.

"Let's get started. " I sat in my director's chair and grabbed my iPhone. Everyone got in their positions.

Camilla took her spot on the queen-size bed in the prop-style bedroom one of my cameramen used a chalkboard and placed it in front of the camera. "Drink from my river, scene six, take two!"

I sat back and watched the movie unfold like a father watching his firstborn enter the world. Roman, whose character's name was Domonique entered the house. Domonique and Camilla's character, Rita had been sending break-up texts back and forth all day.

Rita lay in her bed as she cried herself to sleep. Even though she'd texted Domonique saying she hated him, she could never stop loving him.

Domonique walked into Rita's room. Rita was lying in her bed in the black dress she had put on to go out to dinner with another guy. Admitting to herself that she couldn't move past Dominique, she concealed her date and spent her night crying herself to sleep.

Domonique walked to her bedside. Her shiny ponytail glistened under the bright light. He stared at her as she buried her face in the pillow. Domonique slowly sat at the foot of her bed. He rubbed her toned legs, but she still didn't move. His hand moved to the curve of her ass. He moved his hand under the hem of her dress. Her skin was warm to his touch. She stirred in her sleep but she didn't wake. Now lying on her back, her head to the side, Domonique slid her dress up, just a little.

23

Xtasy

Neyo's song - Mad, played softly as background music.

Baby, I know, sometimes, it's gonna rain / But baby can we make up now cause I can't sleep through the pain.

Rita squirmed again. She blinked her eyes open and said, "Dom!"

Domonique smiled. "How'd you know it was me?"

She lay down facing him. "Because no one's ever touched me the way you touch me."

He slid her dress over her mound. His fingers brushed her entrance. Rita closed her legs trying her hardest to resist his charm. Her body gave in opening to his touch. He played at her entrance, staring into her eyes as she moaned.

"You mean, like this?" he asked, working his fingers faster. Rita's pussy glistened right in front of the camera, and her live audience.

Her eyes closed as he brought his body over hers. His lips were just inches away from hers. He massaged her clit as he spoke softly to her.

"I'm sorry, love. Take me back, this time, forever." he worked his fingers faster.

Rita's legs opened and closed around his hand. Her back arched off the bed, only to be stopped by his chest. "I can't," she panted.

"Why can't you?" he softly asked.

"Because,"

"Because, what?"

"Because … you're going to hurt me again. It might not be today or tomorrow, or next week. But one day, you're going to hurt me."

Domonique kissed her soft lips. His fingers never stopped strumming her clit. I watched as my favorite part was about to come up. It brought a smile to my face. I love my job.

"If I hurt you today, I'm sorry. I'm sorry for tomorrow, and the week after. I'm not perfect, no man is," he kissed her lips, then lightly bit her cheek. She moaned as she humped into his fingers.

Moan in my Mouth

"But if I hurt you, know that I'm hurting too. Because my heart is yours, and yours, mine. When you bleed, I bleed. When you cry, I cry. And when you die, pronounce me dead too, "cause I can never live without you." I mouthed the words as Domonique said them out loud.

"Oh my, Lord!" Rita screamed as Domonique eased his face down her pussy. His fingers were coated with her juices.

I always wanted to know what Camilla tasted like. I never asked her, or Roman. She always ate peaches, so one would think she tasted like peaches.

"I' l - I'll take you back under one condition," she panted.

Domonique looked up from her pussy. "Name it."

"Drink from my river." She said,

Domonique smiled. He lowered his face to her pussy as her river flowed. Rita moaned and moaned as she held onto Domonique's head.

I stood up and shouted. "Cut!" Roman stood up and wiped her juices from his chin. He helped Camilla up as she pulled her dress down.

I looked to the side of me. Karen held my cup of cappuccino in her hand. She shook her head and said, "God, I'm going to miss this place."

$$$

Xtasy

Chapter 4
-Cedrick-

I walked inside of my new job at Bloody Lyrics records. I took a deep breath. I did it the same way Mike Epps did in the movie, Next Friday. I couldn't lie, the air inside Bloody Lyrics, in fact, tastes different. I don't know why, but it did.

I came dressed to impress. I had to, being the new head A&R for the second most popular record company in Texas behind Rap-A-Lot records. I looked sharp in my black and grey Giorgio Armani suit, with a grey Tom Ford tie. My black Tom Ford shoes looked plain, but the $2,200 price tag could give anyone a heart attack.

I was nervous as hell. It was my first day on the job. I worked my ass off my whole life to get to this point in my life. It was nowhere, and like I said, I'm nervous, but I didn't show it. At least I hope I didn't.

"You must be Mr. Montgomery?" A very light-skinned woman with freckles smiled at me with her hand out. I smiled back and shook her hand. She was a very beautiful woman. Slim waist-long curly hair she kept in a curly ponytail puffball.

"Yes, I'm Cedrick Montgomery. But, you can call me Ced." I let her hand go before I took it home with me. Back in my younger days, I would've skipped all of the normal greetings, and skipped to the sexual greeting in the back of my G-Wagon. But, I was a changed man. An engaged man at that.

"My name is Trineka Bridges. I am the public speaker and analyst for Bloody Lyrics records. I can speak for everyone when I say, we're glad to have you here."

"I'm glad to be here." I looked around. The place was nice. Huge, but nice.

"Did you find the place easy enough?" She asked as she stared into my eyes.

I smiled and looked away like a shy teenager. "I did. I used to stay in Dallas a long time ago. Not much has changed since then. In fact, when I was a teen, this same building used to be the auditorium for graduations. It didn't look nearly this good back in the day."

"You are so right. I actually graduated in this same building."

"Me too. What school did you graduate from?"

"Burdner."

"Really. So you're a Ram?"

She smiled. "Yes, that is correct. What about you? Where did you graduate from?"

"Lake Highlands," She gave me a surprised look. "Yes, I know, horrible school, but I was lucky enough to have some very caring teachers that wanted me to go far in life."

"Thank God for them, huh." She smiled, displaying her perfect teeth.

Thank God for your mother, wow! I thought to myself.

A tall, bald head muscular African American man walked up beside Trineka and wrapped his arm around her waist, pulling her close to him, basically putting his stamp on her to let me know she was his.

I smiled. I was no damn fool. The muscular bald man was none other than Jason Woods, my boss. The man whose company and signature will be all over my future checks.

"Mr. Woods, it's a pleasure to meet you. My name is Cedrick Montgomery, I'm your new A&R." I held my hand out.

Jason shook my hand, and he laughed." I thought you were over here trying to steal my fiance."

I looked at Trineka's hand. I hadn't noticed she was wearing a ring on her finger. Back in my younger days, I didn't pay attention to that or care enough to see if a woman had on a ring. I guess old habits do die slow.

I held my left hand up to show them my wedding band. "No sir, I'm also waiting to walk down the aisle with the woman of my dreams." If I wasn't mistaken, Trineka gave my hand a disgusting look.

"Congrats," Jason smiled. "So, did you enjoy the tour? You like what you see so far, your office? Is it big enough?" He asked question after question.

Moan in my Mouth

"No, I-uh. I just recently walked through the door."

"Trineka, what are you waiting on. Show the man around. Let him take in his new place of business. Matter of fact, Franko Zay is in the studio as we speak, he's about to lay down a new track, let him see his new talent."

Trineka turned around. Jason popped her on the ass. I knew it was more for my benefit. "Jay, what did I tell you about doing that in public," she sounded upset.

"Baby, I own the place. Who's going to judge you, huh?" Let me know, and they'll be looking for a new job.

Trineka rolled her eyes. "Mr. Montgomery, if you want to follow me, I'll show you around."

She took the lead. I took frequent glances at her long toned legs. The way they flowed up the bottom of her black leather skirt, to her bubble butt.

"Ced, did you hear me?" Trineka asked. I honestly didn't hear a word he said. Her legs had my undivided attention.

"No, I'm sorry. What did you say?"

"I said, I apologize for the way Jason acted. He sometimes can be-"

"Egotistic," I said.

She smiled. "And sometimes,"

"Obnoxious," I finished her sentence.

She laughed again. "You talk like you know him."

"Well, being in the music industry, I can say that I've met many men like him. But, it's okay, I know how to deal with them."

"Good to know." She stared at me. We stood outside a recording studio that had a red light above the door, indicating that the room was in use. "First stop, our top artist at Bloody Lyrics Franko Zay!"

***

-Franko-

Xtasy

"One time for foreign nation! DJ spoke, turn that shit back, start it all the way over! We don't want toms nothing!" I spoke into the mic.

I stood inside the soundproof booth with a blunt in between the fingers of my left hand. My Glock 40 was lugging my hip like a shy baby. I held my iPhone in my hand as my lyrical words were broadcasted across the screen. I was already on my second cup of crown. The loud pack that I was smoking had my blood flow intune with the sound of the smooth beat.

I thought back to all the days and nights I spent in prison. The abandonment. The betrayal. It was just three months ago that I was released from prison after doing a ten-year bid. I went in as a young hustler. I came out an OG. The penitentiary wasn't the best vacation I've ever experienced, but it was the best school I've ever experienced. The school of hard knock. What I didn't know about the game, I learned it over the ten years I've spent in prison.

As a teen, I picked the pack over a nine to five. Hand over hand, I made over a rack a day. I fed my sister Nae and my brother, Marlon like I was the adult. When I went to prison, my crew abandoned me, right along with my baby mamas, Jas, and Bria.

Prison was a piece of the world I cherished. It was special to me knowing that a lot of people would never get a chance to see the inside of the penitentiary. Not that San Quentin scared straight shit they put on TV. I'm talking about the real penitentiary, what really went on behind the hood gated community.

The shit I saw and did, only the real niggas in the penitentiary will ever understand it. It was like when I was telling other inmates my pains, hurts, and dreams, I wrote them down. For ten years, it was me, my pen, my pad, and my radio. Rappers like Yo Gotti, Money Bagg Yo, Da Baby, Lil Baby, and Young Dolph kept me focused. It was their lyrics that kept me motivated. Their lyrics were a reflection of my lifestyle.

Like Yo Gotti said, I was the G.O.A.T, I felt like I was the greatest at everything I did. Like Young Dolph, I felt that I was bulletproof. Surviving in two different worlds was the way I

Moan in my Mouth

dodged bullets on numerous occasions, niggas shot at me. Even the system tried to take shots at me. Yet I survived. Like Money Bagg Yo, I felt that I was at a relentless stage in my life; I wasn't gon' let shit stop me. Me seeing the true hustle in each rapper is what made me change my hustle. Rapping was my new forte. I was still that same young nigga at heart, wanting every dollar that I felt I deserved. The gangsta in me made me want to go after every dollar I felt the world owed me. And what better way, than to speak to the world, at my own pace, with a smooth contagious beat. For some reason, it was like me, music, and DJ Spoke were joined together at birth by the hip. Music and the truth that came with it are what made me see life with a new set of eyes.

I sipped my Crown Royal as DJ Spoke started the beat from the top. I bobbed my head as I adjusted my beats by Dre headphones on my head. I could feel the smooth beat flowing through my ears.

I closed my eyes and imagined a vivid picture of myself performing in a sold-out show at the Cowboy's stadium. I opened my eyes with pain, anger, and revenge.

"The only way y'all can ever feel my pain is to live the exact life I've lived. Seeing that, that shit ain't possible, I guess I gotta paint a picture for you. But when I'm done, don't look surprised!" Then I went in.

Tell me how you 'pose to lose when yo got God by yo' side / tell me how you 'pose to feel when niggas died by yo' side / nigas flexin' 'bout that smoke, but they know they ain't gon' ride / too much paper for me to get, bitch don't fuck up my vibe / can see the pain in my eyes / on many nights I had to cry / can't believe she tld me lies / thought i would lose, but I won, everybody look surprise / did a lot of soup searching' I'm movin' differently / committed a lot of deadly sins / but my shoes christian / emotionally scared, from my term in the penitentiary / pandemic 3,000 men unit / how the fuck we 'posed to social distance / cherish yo' looks, but after that what an you offer me (nothing) / and you expect me to give you another offspring / tats on my body tellmy

Xtasy

history, my past life / I don't talk, I just step / niggas better get their act right / many occasions, crack and razor ducking flash lights / gold myhitta when he hit 'em, hold that mack tight / she got a nigga, but I hit her, just last night / all I see i soney, thats that bag sight! /

The beat dropped to a slow, smooth treble. I took my headphones off and waved my hand. DJ Spoke killed the beat; he pressed a button on his soundboard and said.
"What happened?"
I shook my head and hit the barely lit blunt. "I wasn't feeling it. Let's do it again."
DJ Spoke laughed. "My nigga, that was the tenth time. Each time, it was perfect. Look, there's somebody out here to see you."
I hung my headphones on the mic stand, grabbed my glass of crown and walked out of the booth. "That was some heat," Trineka said as I hugged her.
"Yeah, that's a fa'sho hit." A man that was standing beside Trineka said.
I sat on the leather couch. "I 'preciate it, but who are you?"
He held his hand out to me. "I'm Cedrick Montgomery, I'm the head of A&R now."
I shook his hand, "What happened to Trent?"
"Trent was fired last month. Did yo forget?" Trineka said.
I laughed. "I never knew that."
" Well, maybe you should start attending the board member meetings." She playfully kicked my foot with her heel.
"So - Cedrick," I started to say before he held his hand up.
"Call me, Ced." He said.
"Ced, What are you planning on doing now that you're the new A&R?"
"I plan on taking you to the next level. Sold out arenas headlining the biggest award show. Commercials, soundtracks, you name it; we're going to do it."

Moan in my Mouth

I nodded and smiled. I like him already. If you were talking money, then you were talking my language. All I understood was ching-ching, and the sound of a money counter beeping.

"I'm with it, ten toes down." I pulled my Glock from my hip and sat it beside me on the arm of the couch. Ced eyed my Glock. "Just so you know, I was a trapper before I became a rapper. I keep my Glock on me to keep my past in the past."

Ced nodded. "I wasn't always an A&R!"

$$$

Xtasy

Chapter 5
-Cupid-

My lips locked with Karen's as she fumbled to get the key inside her door. Her lips tasted almost as sweet as her perfume smelled. It had to be either Fendi or Gucci. The reason I knew was that I took it to heart to learn as much as I could about women, and what they liked.

"What kind of perfume is that you're wearing?" My lips moved to her neck as my curiosity got the best of me.

"Ahh! Fendi!" she moaned.

I knew it, I was rarely wrong. Karen fumbled with the key like she had the wrong house. "You better hurry, I don't want anyone to see us." I urged her on as I slid my hand under the back of her dress. I pinched her soft cheeks, she jumped, her chest hugged the door as I sandwiched her between it.

"Why not? Umph!" She said, then moaned as I parted her legs. "It's not like I work for you anymore. I mean, I did put my two weeks notice in today."

"I noticed." I laughed as we stumbled into her house. I slammed the door and grabbed her by the back of her head bringing her lips to mine." Where's Maria?" I asked.

"She's with my sister. Why?"

"I just had to make sure. I didn't want to scare her."

"Why would she be scared?" She asked.

"When I get inside you, you'll never stop screaming."

Karen pushed me away and smiled. "I've waited a long time for this day." She let her hair pin fall, she shook her head side to side letting her long hair fall over her shoulders. Her hair flowed like a river down her back.

"I'm going to bed. Do you wanna come with me?" she smiled and walked away.

I watched how her ass looked perfect in her tight knee-length dress. My blood pumps through my body, warming places that control my life.

I looked around her house. It was a two-bedroom, but a nice size two-bedroom. She had a nice sectional that took up most of the space in the living room. All of her furniture looked brand new. I didn't know I paid her that much to be able to afford a place like this.

"You coming, or what?" She stood at the bedroom door with a sexy lingerie get-up on. The pink stitching matched the color of her soft lips. The gap between her legs intensified her beauty. Women were amazing, just a change of posture could turn a man on. I know it did for me.

Karen dropped her bra as I took slow steps towards her bedroom. Tossing the bra to me, it felt light. I wondered how something so light could hold a pair of twins that looked juicy and heavy. Karen took slow, sexy steps to her bed. OG poked at the zipper of my pants demanding to be freed. I walked into her bedroom. The lights were dimmed, the mood was set. Slow, passionate music played from her TV.

Freak me baby, ahh yeah, Freak me baby / Let me lick you up and down, till you say stop / Let me play with your body baby, make you real hot /

Karen sat at the edge of the bed. Her titties sat up like a queen at a dinner table. "Karen, I don't want to hurt you," I said as I took slow steps toward her.

"Cupid, I'm grown. I understand what this is. It's just meaningless sex, I understand."

I shook my head. "That's not what I'm talking about." I unbuttoned each button on my shirt slowly as I stared into her eyes. I was a real man. I didn't just bump and grind, I had passionate sex. Fucking went by too fast for me. I needed at least ten minutes of foreplay to really get going. Plus, I've never been a selfish person, I made sure the woman I played with got hers before I got mine.

I tossed my shirt to the floor. This time, I made sure to keep a mental note of where I tossed it. I pulled my wife-beater over my head, tossing it beside my shirt.

"Wow!" Karen said as she ran her nails down my six-pack.

Moan in my Mouth

"You haven't seen anything yet." I undid my belt, and Karen clasped her hand over mine.

"Please! Let me. She took my belt from its loops, then folded the belt. She placed one end to the other, then she pulled it quickly making a pop noise. She giggled, then eased my pants down, the whole time she stared into my eyes. Her stare was intoxicating. I wondered if she could match that stare when OG made his way inside of her.

OG poked at my briefs, Karen pulled them down, OG sprung up like he had a spring built in him. "Oh, God!" Karen said.

I smiled at her reaction. "So, you two have met?"

"What, the, hell, is, that?"

"That, my dear, is oh God. But you can call him, OG."

"I - Its -." She stuttered.

"It's a penis, I know. Ever seen one before?"

"This size, only on pornos. It's -"

"Unbelievable, huh," I said.

She nodded. She fumbled with the head of OG. She was excited, yet nervous. She bit her lip, her head moved to the side, deciding which way she wanted to come at OG. OG moved his head with hers, like a cobra. She leans her head forward, her hair falls around her shoulders. The head of OG enters her mouth. I didn't warn her about the last woman who failed, I just let her do her thing.

Karen sucks hard. She closed her eyes her dimples shows as she works her jaws around OG. "Don't forget to breathe." I teased. She laughed with a mouth full of OG.

I love when women give me head. Not that mediocre head. But a real deal blow job. Karen, she knew what she was doing. She stared at the length of OG as she worked him down her throat. OG bent at the base as he touched the back of her throat.

Karen withdrew her mouth and inhaled deep. "Ahh! you like that?"

"Why'd you stop?"

37

Xtasy

"Because," she said, her hand moving up and down OG in a circular motion. "You're not my boss anymore. I'm the boss now. What I say, goes." She released OG and stood up.

I took a step back, giving her space between me, and the bed. She turns her back to me. I grab a hold of her neck from the back and pull her to me.

"I'll always be the boss of you, especially after tonight." her body is flushed with mine. I grab a hold of her left nipple and pulled it. She yelps out in pain, but it soon turns into pleasure as I lightly, and gently massaged it.

My nose brushes her ear, then moves down her neck. She smells fresh, ripe. I place soft, tender kisses down her neck. She squirmed under my touch. Her breathing changes. She sounds anxious, nervous, and wanting.

Karen reaches between us, OG snakes between the back of her legs. She reached under him and plays with his twin brothers.

"You like?" I mimicked her as I gently bit her ear.

"Sss, yes-ss! It's big. Sooo, big." I trail kisses from her ear to her neck, and across her shoulder.

"You think you're ready for him?" I asked.

"Ch-check. Ahh, your lips," She moaned. "Check and, ohh, see."

I hooked my finger in her victoria secret panties. My thumb grazed her cum coated lips. She was definitely ready. I eased her panties down her legs, we both stepped out of our last piece of loathing at the same time.

"Get yo' sexy ass on the bed. Now! She didn't hesitate as she climbed onto the bed with her knees.

As soon as her ass popped out, I reared back and slapped her hand on her left cheek. I'm talking about hard. She looked back in shock. I climbed on the bed behind her. I grabbed her by her long silky hair, her neck jerked as she positioned herself on her knees.

I forced her head into her pillow, and her legs spread willingly. Her flower blossomed and dripped like flowers in April. I grabbed OG and lined him up with her box. She felt the head of OG at her entrance and rocked back into him.

OG found her center, her walls stretched around him. "Damn, what the -" I smacked her ass again, stopping whatever she was about to say.

Karen bucked into me, forcing OG halfway inside her tight walls. As soon as she felt him hit her walls, she jumped halfway across the bed. I laughed, stroking her juices around the undisputed champ. Karen stared at OG as she kept her distance.

"What's wrong?" I asked, smiling.

She shook her head and said. "You named your dick, oh God. What you should've named him, was what the fuck!"

$$$

Xtasy

Chapter 6
-Cedrick-

Friday came back around so quickly. I was honestly happy though, I was in need of a break. Between work, and coming home to unpack, I was exhausted. Thank God Amy and I finally finished unpacking. I don't know who was more excited, me or her. I think I took the cake, being that I was happy I could host the first fella's night at my house.

Amy made over twenty turkey finger sandwiches and bought three twenty-four cases of Bud Light Platinum and a bunch of different snacks. I told her it was only my close friends, Cupid, Nemo, and Samuel. We all had been close friends since grade school.

Nemo, whose real name is Neimon, reminds me of the Comedian, Dave Chappelle, but Nemo still has hair. Nemo's a very laid-back guy. He never goes out of his way to get in anyone's business. Nemo was a hustler. Not a dope pusher, but a true hustler. He had his own personal delivery service. He could get anything you needed, flowers, clothes, phones, whatever. He could get it for you, and one of them would be boosted. Nemo had been delivering people's orders to their doorway before Amazon, if only he would've known the power and demand of his trade.

Samuel, whole we nicknamed uncle Sam because he was the oldest was the outspoken one out of the group. He was the real hustler out of the group. Unlike Nemo, uncle Sam sold narcotics. Not the street dope, like cocaine, heroin, or crack. Nah, uncle Sam sold behind-the-counter drugs. Codeine Syrup, Percocets, Ambien, Rolof and he sold Viagra and Cialis. Uncle Sam was smart though. Too smart to be selling drugs if you ask me.

After the fella's was introduced to Amy, I led them down to the basement, the man cave. The looks they gave Amy when they saw her were priceless; I knew I had a very beautiful fiance. I liked when other men noticed it too.

It felt good to sit around the poker table with my guys as I dealt out a hand of Texas Hold 'em.

Xtasy

"Ced, now that you're working at Bloody Lyrics, I know you gon' bless me with all the new music before it drops in the stores. That way, I can sell them on the street for double the cover price." Nemo was always thinking of a way to get the extra dollar.

I tossed two single dollars on the poker table in the pot, raising the bet to two dollars. Cupid threw his cards in. "Fold," Cupid said, twisting the cap off his third beer.

"You know I can't do that, Nemo. They'll fire me," I said. Uncle Sam tossed his cards in. "I fold too," he said.

I looked at Nemo to see what he would do, he looked at me and tossed his two dollars in the pot. " raise you, another buck." he said and smiled.

I looked at the cards that were laid out on the table, then at the ones in my hand. There was a two of clubs, a five of diamond, a six of hearts, a king of spades, and a ten of clubs. In my hand, I had two kings. I looked at Nemo, wondering what cards he held in his hand. Nemo had never been good at poker or bluffing. We've been playing this game since we were kids, only back then, we played for marbles. Today, it seemed like Nemo held a mask over his face because I couldn't read him.

"I call," I said, tossing another dollar in the pot. Nemo flipped his cards out exposing his three of hearts, and four of spades.

I shook my head and tossed my two measly kings on the table. Nemo pulled his money in and smiled. That was the first hand he's won in over ten years. Cupid downed his third beer then reached for another one.

"Damn Cupid, let me find out you turned into an alcoholic since I've been away," I said as Amy walked down the stairs with a platter of finger sandwiches, a side of chips, and a center of dips. She was looking every bit of the way she did when I first laid eyes on her, beautiful.

"Thought yo gentleman would have worked up an appetite or lost one." Amy smiled as she laid the platter on the bar.

"Thanks Amy," Nemo said, on the verge of standing up.

Moan in my Mouth

"Oh no Nemo. Sit," Amy said. "I got you guys. Y'all enjoy your night." Nemo sat back down, I smiled at Amy. I was happy to call her mine.

"So Cupid. Back to you, what's the deal? Why the long face?" I asked.

"I'm not an alcoholic. I just got something on my mind."

"Like what?" I asked.

"My secretary put in her two weeks' notice. She's been with me since the beginning. It's going to be hard to replace her. Hell, it's already hard to replace her. I'm lost, and it's only been three days," he sighed. "She's still with me for the moment until the two-week notice is up, but I already can tell it's going to be hard to replace her."

"Come on, it ain't gon' be that hard to find another secretary. Hell, you're the owner of a multi-million dollar company," Nemo said as he bit into one of Amy's famous finger sandwiches. "Umm, this is really good, Amy." Nemo wasn't just sucking up, Amy could make a sandwich taste like a steak.

"Thanks Nemo. I have plenty if you want more." She grabbed four fresh beers and sat them in front of us. Cupid downed the one he'd just opened then twisted the cap on the one Amy sat in front of him.

"I don't want just any woman, Ced. She has to be smart, dependable, and a people person, not mistakenly, she has to be professional. Karen, she made my job easy. I paid her well, but she worked for every dime."

"It won't be that hard Cupid, just look around. Nowadays, you can post that you're looking for a secretary online, and they'll come to you." Uncle Sam pointed out.

"I suppose you sell your narcotics online too?" Nemo teased. We all laughed.

"Watch it, Dave Chappelle lookin' boy." Uncle Sam joked. Amy laughed from behind us. I had forgotten she was still in the room.

"Amy, you laughing at me?" Nemo said as Amy covered her mouth to stop laughing.

43

Xtasy

"I'm sorry, but you kinda look like him, a little." She laughed.

"No you didn't, Akwafina lookin' ass." Nemo cracked at Amy.

Amy laughed, then scrunched up her face. "That was a low blow. I do not look like her."

I pulled Amy close to me. "Get off my baby. She looks way better than Akwafina." I kissed her on the cheek.

I looked at Cupid as he took his beer to the head.

"Cupid!" He looked at me. "What about Amy?" I looked at Amy

"What about me?" She asked.

"You could be his secretary, that is until he can find a permanent one."

Amy looked at Cupid. Cupid looked at me like I was crazy.

"Ced, you do know where I work, don't you? Or have you forgotten?" Cupid asked.

"Oh, I know. But it's not like she'll be on the film or production team. She'll only be doing paperwork and answering the phone, right?" I wasn't really sure what his secretary did. I just hated to see my guy down. I figured Amy was probably bored sitting in the house all day every day.

"Where do you work?" Amy asked. Sam and Nemo both started laughing. Amy looked at them and asked. "What's so funny?"

"Cupid owns a porn industry -" I tried to explain before Cupid cut me off.

"Not just any porn industry," Cupid said. "I own the number one professional porn industry. Pandora's Poison is known all across the globe for our hit movies."

Amy's mouth was wide open. "So, you're a porn star?" She asked.

Cupid laughed. "In my own home, I am. But, no. I'm the owner and the scriptwriter. I have my own actors who start in the movies."

Moan in my Mouth

"And Ced, you're fine with me working at a porn industry?" Amy asked.

"Well, it's not entirely up to me, it's up to Cupid. I mean, he's the boss, he has to hire you."

Cupid looked at me. I knew he was probably upset at me for putting him under the gun like that. Amy looked at Cupid as Cupid tossed the idea around in his head. He looked at Amy and said.

"We have a strict dress code. Casual dress Mondays through Thursday. Friday is considered jean day. Off days are weekends, you'll start training tomorrow."

A smile crept on Amy's face. She kissed my cheek excitedly and said." Thanks Cupid. Oh my God, I got a job. I promise I'll be on time every day, and you won't regret it. You'll want to hire me permanently." She smiled, then ran back up the stairs.

I shook my head and laughed. "Why'd you do that Ced?" Cupid asked me.

"What?"

'You know what," Cupid said. "You knew I wouldn't tell her no. She's not going to like it."

"You said it's a professional film industry. She'll like it, watch. Plus, it'll give you two time to get to know each other. It's a win-win. That way she has a job, and she can stop nagging me about being bored at home."

"You got any more openings, my wife needs a job, too." Nemo joked.

Cupid laughed and threw his beer top at Nemo.

$$$

Xtasy

Chapter 7
-Amy-

I woke up early to cook Ced and me some breakfast before we both headed our separate ways to work. It felt good to say that I had a job. Ced didn't really like me to work. Once he found out he was the A & R for Bloody Lyrics Records, he made me quit my job. I loved Ced dearly, but I didn't like depending on him to take care of me. I was my own woman, that's why this job was so important to me.

I smiled the entire time I cooked breakfast. I cooked two pieces of wheat toast and placed them on the plate beside two sunny side-up eggs. I pulled four pieces of turkey bacon from the skillet and placed them on Ceds plate beside his toast. I fixed him a cup of Folgers coffee with two spoons of sugar, along with his favorite snickers creamer.

Ced walked into the kitchen as he was fixing his tie. "Morning beautiful! What smells so good?" He asked as he kissed me on the cheek.

"Nothing too special. Just something to get the day started. Eggs, toast, and a few pieces of bacon," I sat his plate in front of him along with his cup of coffee.

"Thanks bae," he smiled and looked at me. "You look beautiful. You ready for your first day?"

I sat across from him with my plate." As ready as I'll ever be, I guess."

I dressed professional like Cupid instructed. I wore my black leather, Fendi skirt that stopped right at my knees. My black and white H & M button-down matched my black and white Vince Camuto high heels. I wanted to look the part.

"You'll be the shadow for the first few days, learning the ins and outs basically getting the feel of things."

I nodded as I took a bite of my toast. I closed my eyes as I savored the buttery bread. I always used it; I can't believe it's not butter. Sometimes I will be shocked that it's really not butter.

"You think he'll put me on permanently?" I asked as I sat my toast back down. I stood up and grabbed two glasses from the shelf. I can't believe I forgot the orange juice.

As I opened the refrigerator, Ced said. "I think he will."

"Why, 'cause I'm his best friend's fiance?" I poured us both a glass and returned the juice.

"That, and, you're going to show him you deserve the position." He said as I sat his cup in front of him and took my seat.

We ate and talked as Ced kept smiling at me. "Why do you keep smiling at me like that?" I blushed.

"Because. You, you look beautiful. Like how I first met you at Starbucks. You remember?"

I blushed. "How could I forget. You forced me to have coffee with you." I laughed, thinking back to the day.

We both finished eating, I grabbed our plates and rinsed them before sticking them in the dishwasher along without glasses. I wiped the countertop clean as I felt Ced hug me from the back.

"You know, we've been so busy, that we haven't broken our new house in," he placed soft kisses all over my neck as he gripped my hips.

I smiled as I gave him my neck as if he was a vampire. "We did say we would break every room in, didn't we."

He kissed my cheek, pinning me between the counter. "We sure did."

"After work, if you're not so tired." I joked. Ced's hands went up the back slit of my skirt. I parted my legs to give him a little feel.

"I can't wait that long," he panted as his fingers moved my Victoria Secret thang to the side. His fingers pushed inside of my box. I was Asian, so my pussy was tight and wet. With his other hand, he raised my shirt above my juicy ass. I could feel him kneeling down behind me.

"We were going to be late," I moaned as I felt his warm breath against my ass cheeks.

"Well let's make it quick. Arch your back a little." He demanded.

Moan in my Mouth

I did as instructed. I leaned over the counter and arched my back a little making my flower blossom. His warm, wet tongue found my center. His tongue darted in and out of my pussy. It felt so good like he was trying to get all of my juices from my center. I could feel him hooking his tongue at the tip.

"Damn, your tongue bae. Ohh, shit! It's on my ... spot!" I damn near knocked the toaster off the counter as I felt him spread my ass cheeks.

Ced ran his tongue from my pussy, to my asshole in one swift motion. He stood up and fumbled with his belt. His pants dropped to the floor, he sandwiched me between the counter and pinned his dick up with my hole.

"Give it to me, Ced. We're running out of time!" I basically begged for the dick. He taught me, beggers can't be choosers ….. the way he slammed his dick home.

"Umph! Fuck bae!" I moaned as his dick hit rock bottom.

"Damn, it's so wet. Tight, and -uhh, fuck. Gushy!" Ced pushed my ass higher as he dug into my guts.

"Just, for you, dad-dee!"

"I love this pussy! Shit, I love it!" Ced said as his strong hands gripped my hips tighter. I knew what that meant, he was on the verge of cumming.

"Cum, cum in , bae, oh God, cum in me right here in our kitchen," I moaned. I felt him pound in me hard like fifteen times, then his warm semen shot spurts deep inside of my slippery box. Just the feel of his dick pulsating inside of me caused me to cum, too.

We stayed sandwiched together as Ced nudged his chin on my neck. "I may need another shower," he said as we shared a laugh.

***

-Cupid-

Xtasy

I walked into my spacious office and closed the door as soon as I walked in. Karen wasn't at her desk, which was good. I was trying my best to avoid her for what happened the other night. It wasn't like she was the first woman that I fucked that worked - past tense, worked for me. Karen was just the first woman that I fucked, well we didn't really fuck, because as soon as I placed OG inside of her, she ran like a track star.

But, Karen was the first one I fucked, and still had to walk past at work. I know, it's only for two weeks. Ten days to be exact. But knowing OG, it'll be a hard ten days. Cause just the brief feel of her pussy felt like a little piece of heaven.

I closed the blinds to my office, which everyone knew meant that I didn't want to be bothered. I locked the door and placed my suit jacket on the coat rack. I walked to my adjoining restroom and opened the door.

"Karen!" I took a step back as she walked towards me naked, except for her high heels that made her look ready and willing. Exotic like.

She backed me all the way to my desk. I scurried around it and ended up sitting in my chair. "Where're your clothes, Karen?" I admit, yes I asked the question, but I couldn't help but stare at her sexy lips. They were juicy, and fat at the tip, like she had applied lip gloss to them. Slightly parted, as if she'd just taken her finger from out of them.

"Please, Cupid. Let me try again," She straddles my lap. As she adjusted herself, I noticed her cream on my knee.

"Karen, we can, but not here, not now. My best friend's wife will be here soon. You have to get ready to train her," I tried to lift her up, but she held her weight down on my lap.

Karen went for my belt, then my zipper. "Give me two minutes, I just want to feel you inside of me again. Since you put your dick inside me, it seems like there's been a hole there that only you can fill."

My fingers moved to her slit, she was super wet, dripping. Her juices made a puddle on my lap. I couldn't help myself. I played with her pussy as she humped my fingers. OG strained against my

Moan in my Mouth

pants demanding to be freed. OG was a jealous bastard, never one to be left out of the fun.

"SS-Stop teasing me, and give me what I-I want, please!" Karen begged.

I picked her up and sat her on top of my desk, her legs fell open. I pulled my pants down as she sucked her cum coated fingers. My pants dropped, and my briefs shimmied down my legs. OG posed for the camera. I stroked OG, massaging his head like a good dog.

"I'm not letting you run this time. I'm already breaking one of my rules for your sexy ass."

"Punish this pussy, make me pay for breaking the rules. I need it, please!"

Her moans did it for me. I leaned down and kissed her neck. OG crawled into her slippery hole with no assistance. "Uhm, that's it, daddy! Stretch my tight pussy. Fuck!" Karen screamed as I slid deeper inside of her tight pussy. She screamed so loud that I had to cover her mouth with my hand.

OG was halfway in, and halfway out. Karen humped into me as if she was ready to take all of OG inside of her. I slid inside a little more, her eyes shot open as she bit down on the palm of my hand. She placed the palm of her hand on my shirt making sure I didn't go hard on her pussy.

"Scary ass," I smiled. "I knew you weren't ready. You were just bumping."

Karen's eyes turned into slits as she bit her lip. Her lil sexy ass had some sexy fuck faces; like she was auditioning for a role in one of my films.

"More," she moaned.

"You sure?"

She nodded and bit her lip. I took a slow step as OG started closing the gap between us. "Umhh, fuck! It's too big," she placed her hand on my shirt as she tried to push me out of her juicy pussy.

I grabbed her hands and raised them above her head. I took another step closer. It was like OG was eating at her pussy. "Oh shit, stop!" She begged.

51

Before I could stop, she screamed. "Fuck, it feels so-ooo good!" She bit her lip seductively. "Oh fuck, it hurts so good."

I took another slow step, OG touched the back of her walls, "Cupid, fuck! Dammit-tt!" She screamed. "Give it all to me, make me a woman! Make me a grown-ass woman!"

I filled her pussy to the hilt. I still had maybe two inches that couldn't fit, but she had managed to take as much as her pussy would allow.

"Umhh, fuck! Now fuck me Cupid. Please!" She begged.

I rocked my hips in a circular motion as she clawed at my shirt. She grabbed a hold of my tie and brought my face to hers. She tried to kiss me, but I dodged her lips like Alvin Kamara does a tackle. I grabbed her legs and lifted them above her head. Her pussy grew fatter right before my eyes. Her lips looked swollen, pink, and soaked with her juices. Her pussy was shaved bald, smooth. I spanked her pretty pussy right on her clit.

"Oh God!" She moaned as I did it again, and again.

"Fuck, K-Karen! You got a beautiful pussy." I said as I leaned forward and sucked on her nipples. Her body arched into mine. I plunged OG all the way into her tight pussy, forcing her walls to take all of OG in.

"Fuc-k-k-k! Ah-Ah, fuck!" She moaned as she grabbed my shirt, locking it in her hand.

I snatched away from her grip and spanked her bald pussy harder. I watched as OG worked in and out of her pussy. Her cream coated OG, I spanked her clit, harder, and faster.

"Oh shit, I-I'm, oh God, fu-ckk me-eee!" She moaned as I continued spanking her clit.

"I-I'm, cumming!" She squirted all over my shirt. I smiled, then held my mouth wide open to catch her sweet juices. I slipped OG out and played with her pearl, working my fingers faster and faster on her clit.

Karen squirted and squirted, shooting her cum into my mouth like target practice. "Uhh, fuck-kk! Um, ahh, uh, uh, uh!" She panted as her body spasmed.

Moan in my Mouth

I opened my mouth to let her see all the cum I caught. I let it drip from my mouth to OG as I rained her cum on the head and shined hi like a new set of tires. I grabbed her legs as they spasmed in my hands, I dragged her to the edge of the desk. Karen shook her head. "N-No, more. I-I can't take no more."

Just as I was about to place OG at her entrance a knock came at my office door.

"Cupid, it's Amy!"

$$$

Xtasy

Chapter 8
Trineka

I cradled the artist files in my hand as I stood outside Cedrick's office door. I double-checked my appearance up and down. I couldn't figure out why, because I was engaged, and so was Cedrick. I had to be honest with myself, he was very attractive, the ideal man. Tall, brown-skinned, and handsome. He was smart, and he had an ear for talent. Plus, he looked damn good in a suit. In some ways, Cedrick reminded me of my fiance, Jason. Before Jason became a multi-millionaire.

When I first met Jason, he was my ideal man. He made all of my dreams come true. He showered me with love, affection, and diamonds. He was there for me physically, and emotionally. But it seems like ever since I said yes to his proposal, the only time I see him is when he wants to walk the red carpet, or when he wants some pussy. I never downplay my punanny. I know I have some bomb ass pussy. But lately, Jason's been either too tired or too busy to get any. I ain't nobody's fool. The only time a man gets tired of good pussy, is when he gets some new pussy.

I turned the knob, opening the door to his office. His back was turned to me as he stood on his chair to hang up a picture of him and Jay-Z. I waited until he was finished. He stopped down and smiled once he saw it was me.

"Trineka, what a pleasant surprise," he walked towards me. Can I get you anything to drink, water, orange juice?" He walked to his mini-fridge.

I smiled, seeing how happy he was to finally have his spacious office in order. "I'm fine, I just came by to drop off some files."

"Oh yea, what kind?" He licked his lips like LL Cool J. My clit pulsated, I could feel it.

"Just some files from the artist. You know, their progress over the years. Their number ones and top one hundreds. Just a little something to get you caught up on who's who."

Xtasy

"Let me check it out," I handed the files to him. He took them and looked through the top folder.

"Have a seat, I want to ask you a few things," I sat down in one of his nice black leather chairs. I crossed my legs as he walked in front of me and sat on the edge of his desk, facing me. His dick print sat on his leg clear as day. I stared at his print as he looked through the files.

"What's up with, Belofante? I haven't heard him drop a single in a while."

"Uhm, he's been in the studio, he recently got married, so he's been at home a lot with his new bride and son."

Cedrick smiled. "Seems like everyone's getting married, huh," he said as he looked at the huge diamond on my finger.

I smiled back. It was a half-smile so he couldn't see the hurt I was good at hiding. "You're right. I guess cupids are on a love spree this year."

Cedrick laughed. "Crazy that you say that. My best friend's name is Cupid. He doesn't believe in love, only sex and lust."

"Wow! Som' friend. What is he, a pimp?" I joked.

"Close. He's a multi-million dollar owner of a professional porn film industry called Pandora's Poison."

"Oh, wow!" I looked at Cedrick and wondered what it would be like if I and him were to make a porn together. I lowered my head and smiled at the thought.

"So, have you and Jason found a date yet?" He asked.

"Huh?"

"You and Jason. Have you two picked a date yet?"

"Oh, well we've been talking about it, but he's left it up to me."

"Same here. I left it all up to my fiance, Amy."

"Amy. That's the lucky lady's name?" I looked at him. "Let me guess, she's white?"

He laughed. "Why would you say that?"

"Only because every brother that comes up in life always leaves the sisters behind to go to the land of the once forbidden."

Moan in my Mouth

"Well, she's not white, but she's also not black. She's Asian. And I'm not marrying her to get back at the sisters. Believe me when I say, I've met some amazing sisters, but Amy, she took the cake."

For some reason, I felt a tinge of jealousy in my stomach. I wondered if Jason talked about me like that when I wasn't around.

"Amy's a lucky woman. If she's smart, she'll rush you down the aisle." I said what I felt and stood up. I walked to his office door.

"Trineka, wait!" His baritone voice sent chills down my spine. You're engaged, Trin', remember. I reminded myself.

I faced him, his sinister smile warmed my blood. "Do you want to go out for some coffee? Maybe you can lace me up on what' what." He walked over to me and whispered. "Because honestly, I'm nervous. I don't want to mess this up."

I smiled, well blushed. "Sure, but it'll be my treat."

Cedrick grabbed his suit jacket and car keys. "What I told you, let's keep that as our little secret. I don't want your fiance to think he hired an unfit A&R manager."

I huffed, why did he have to bring Jason up? "On second thought, Cedrick, I almost forgot that I had to prepare a speech for, uh-an artist," I told a bald-faced lie. "So, I'll have to grab that coffee with you some other time."

Cedrick laid his expensive suit jacket on the arm of his chair as his smile faded. I prayed he couldn't read through my bullshit excuse for dodging him.

"Okay, uh." He stuttered. "That's understandable. Raincheck, uh." He brought his signature smile back.

I nodded and scurried out of his office. Once I knew he wasn't behind me, I placed my back on the wall and closed my eyes.

"There you are-" Jason said, startling me. "Grab Mr. Montgomery, tell him we're having a board meeting in the conference room in the next ten minutes."

I nodded. As I began to walk off, Jason patted me on the ass. I stopped and closed my eyes. He was really starting to piss me the hell off!

***

-Cedrick-

"Thank you all for being here," Jason said as he stood up to address the room. "I called this meeting so that I can properly introduce a man that I know you've all heard of before. He's the new head of our A&R, and he's the man that's going to help us sign some new talent, and sharpen the talent we already have. Without further ado, Mr. Cedrick Montgomery!"

I smiled as I stood up to the round of applause the room brought. I buttoned my suit jacket and silently cleared my throat.

"Thank you, ladies and gentlemen of the board. Thank you Mr. Woods for hiring me, and for putting your trust, and money behind me." I looked around the room. Everyone in attendance was equally important.

"Mr. Woods said a mouthful, I am here to bring this company, Bloody Lyrics, new talent. I am also here to make sure the artists we have, prosper, and become the artists we know they can be." My eyes landed on Belofante.

"Belofante, congrats on the new marriage. You don't know this, but I'm a big fan of yours," Belofante smiled and sat up in his seat.

"You know what a fan hates about having a favorite singer, or rapper?" I asked Belofante.

"Bad publicity," Belofante answered.

"That, and, when an artist takes a long time to put out some hot, new music." Belofante nodded. "Now, I know you have some hits in you, you just have to put in the necessary work." He nodded again.

Moan in my Mouth

"Franko, I listened to one of your studio sessions earlier, you have the fire in you that will set the world ablaze." Franko nodded as he rubbed his beard.

"Today's real artists are being pushed aside for Tik Tok artists. Overnight sensations are filling up stadiums fast, you know why?" I asked no one in particular. "Because they're hungry. They have yet to sign on the dotted line, so they're hungry. Nowadays, it seems like when an artist gets a deal, they lose their ambition, their spunk." I walked around the room, looking every artist in the eyes.

"I came here to help each and every one of you become a Grammy award winner. But, I am not here to be your friend. That's why Trent was fired; instead of trying to help you all make hits, he was busy trying to make friends. I, am not, here, to make friends, only hits. I have a family to feed, as I know most of you do as well."

I looked at Trineka, I had to make sure I thanked her again for the artist files." I had the liberty to look through each and every artist file. Being honest, I am not impressed. This company, Bloody Lyrics, has not had a number one single since Franko's debut album."

I looked at Franko. "Being an artist is more than club appearances and club fights. After all the lawsuits, and legal fees, a regular artist is broke. Look at Bow Wow Kid sensation, he had hit after hit, after hit. Look at him now. We aren't has been records, we're Bloody Lyrics records. From this moment forward, we'll be putting out blood, sweat, and tears into this company. If we all do that, by this time next year, every artist here would have at least two number ones."

I walked back to my seat and unbuttoned my suit jacket.

"Thank you," I said before sitting down.

The room erupted in applause. As I looked over at Trineka, she was smiling and clapping.

$$$

Xtasy

Chapter 9
-Amy-

"Good morning Miss," a dark-skinned doorman greeted me as he held the door to Pandora's Poison open.

"Good morning. Uh, I'm looking for Cupid Patterson. Is his office located here?" I asked.

The doorman smiled. "Yes, Mr. Patterson's office is here. In fact, he owns the entire building," the doorman held his hand out like the models do on The Price is Right.

"Oh, wow." I looked at the large building. "The whole building, really?"

The doorman nodded and smiled. "Yes, I've been with him since he was filming out of his garage, and selling DVDs from his trunk," he looked at me. "Are you going to be working here?" He asked.

I shook my head defensively. "No! I mean, yes. I am, but not in film. I'm going to be his temporary secretary." I don't know why I got so defensive.

"Karen's leaving?" He asked.

"I think she put in her two weeks' notice. Do you know her?" He seemed like he enjoyed opening and closing the doors.

"Oh yes, she's been around a while too. Mr. Patterson has this place run like a family more than a business. Even though I'm only the doorman, he includes me in all the business meetings."

I smiled. "Good to know. So, which floor is his office actually on?"

"The first floor. When you go in, make a right, you'll see it straight ahead." He pointed out.

"Thank you-" I didn't know his name.

"Call me Chad." He smiled.

"Amy," I shook his gloved hand.

Chad held the door open for me. A fresh scent hit my nose as soon as I walked inside. The smell was a mix of strawberry and Kiwi. It smelled amazing.

Xtasy

"Welcome to Pandora's Poison." A beautiful Caucasian woman smiled from behind a counter.

I didn't stop as I continued to my destination. Cupid's office was in plain sight. From the outside of his office, it looked pretty big. I imagined it would be huge, considering he owned the whole building. I walked to his secretary's desk, the desk I'll be using, temporarily, unless he decides to hire me full time.

The desk was vacated. There wasn't a fresh cup of coffee on the desk, or a jacket hanging from the back of the chair indicating that someone was there. I looked to Cupid's office, his door was closed, and the blinds were down. I could hear movement from the inside of his office.

I knocked lightly on the door. "Cupid, it's Amy!" The noise on the inside ceased.

"One minute!" Cupid's voice screamed through the glass windows.

I nodded like he could see me. Maybe five minutes passed before the door opened. A Hispanic woman walked out of his office with a glow on her face. She was pretty. Cupid walked out behind her and closed his door. He had a look of embarrassment written all over his face.

"Amy, glad you could make it. We," he looked at the smiling Hispanic woman. "We were just talking about you." Cupid touched the Hispanic woman on the shoulder, she practically melted under this touch.

"Karen this is Amy, Amy this will be the woman to train you." Karen looked at me, her smile faded.

Karen turned and faced Cupid. She whispered," so this is the woman who's replacing me?" She tried to whisper, but I could hear every word she said.

"She's temporarily taking our spot until I can find a permanent assistant." He tried to whisper also.

"No, I'll stay then." She said.

He shook his head as he placed both hands on her shoulders.

"You can't," He said.

"Why not?" She asked.

Moan in my Mouth

"You know why. It just won't work. Now, behave or you'll never see OG again." Whoever OG was, had to mean a lot to Karen because she got her act together.

"Amy, right!" She plastered a big fake smile on her face. "Welcome to Pandora's Poison, you'll love it here. Care to let me show you around?"

"Sure." I looked at Cupid, he was stressed about something.

"If you follow me," Karen stood in my path of Cupid.

I didn't know what her problem was, but I could tell off the bat, she didn't like me. Call it a woman's intuition, but I sensed.

Karen walked me around the first floor, introducing me to all of the staff. On the first floor was a gift shop, which was full of adult sex toys, DVDs of Pandoras Poison production and cardboard cutouts of all the famous porn stars.

"So, Amy." Karen looked at me with a raised eyebrow. "How do you know Cupid?"

"I - uhm. He's my fiance's best friend and best man." I was curious as to why she wanted to know. "Why?" I asked. I could see by the way she looked at me that she was in love with Cupid.

She finally smiled. "Oh, you're getting married to his best friend. Cedrick, right?"

I nodded. "How'd you know?"

She blushed and said. "I know everything about Cupid." I looked at her sideways as she said it. She finally noticed and said. "It's a part of the job. Cupid, he's very picky, and precise. You'll see."

"If I may, what made you decide to leave. It seems like you like it here?"

She seemed sad as I asked the question like she was regretting her decision to leave. "I wanted to do something different with my life. I have a daughter. I felt like I had to try something different, finish my education, be a good role model for her."

I nodded as she continued. "I love it here. Pandora's Poison is a place that leaves me satisfied in so many ways. The vibe, the atmosphere, the culture, my co-workers, I'ma miss it all. I've been

63

Xtasy

here since the beginning, and it's going to hurt to not be here-," she paused as if she was holding back tears.

"You can always come back once you finish school right?" She shook her head and laughed. "Maybe before, but not anymore. Once I was introduced to OG, my fate at Pandora's Poison was sealed."

"I kinda overheard Cupid bring the phrase up. Who's OG?" I asked curiously.

She smiled. "OG, uhh" she sighed as if she was imagining something. "I'll just say, I hope you never meet OG."

***

-Trineka-

Knock! Knock! I knocked on Jason's office door. After the board meeting, Jason left quickly to his office. He had this look on his face like something was bothering him.

"Who is it?" Jason asked with his signature deep voice.

"It's me," I said as I heard the locks turn and the door swung open. Jason walked away leaving me to close the door.

"Are you okay babe?" I asked as I closed the door and locked it. Jason sat down in his chair and sighed.

"What do you think of Mr. Montgomery?"

"What do you mean?"

"I know I hired him for his resume, but he's been working on the west coast. The music out here is way different from the east coast, especially down south. The south is taking over with the music. In Memphis, you have Yo Gotti, Young Dolph, Black Youngsta, Big 30, Key Glock, Finesse 2sx, and Money Bagg Yo. In Atlanta, you have the Migo's, Gucci Mane, Lil Baby, Future, Young Thug, and Pooh Shiesty, even though he's from Memphis. Then you have Texas altogether. Yella Beezy and Trap Boi Freedy are making headlines, and Bloody Lyrics are supporting has-beens and ex-cons."

Moan in my Mouth

"So what, do you think you've made a mistake by hiring him?"

Jason shook his head as I walked up to him. He pulled me down to his lap." I don't doubt the man has an ear for talent, I just hope he can find the right sound for the label. The brand we're building, it has to be different, Bloody, like our name."

"Babe, I think you just have to give him some time love. He just got here, nothing happens overnight. I think you made a very smart investment. You just have to trust the process."

"You sound like you have a lot of faith in this man. What has he shown you that I haven't seen?"

"Nothing. I just trust your instinct. You didn't hire him to have regrets. What's going on that you're having second guesses?" Jason sighed. "Nothing. Bloody Lyrics is our life. It's our future, and our kids' future." I smiled as he brought up kids. He knew how long I'd been waiting to have kids. Every time I've brought the topic up, he shies away from it. He always brings up how important I am to the company, getting pregnant would keep me away from work.

"You're speaking about our kids' future like we have any."

"Why'd you say it like that?"

I faced him on his lap. "Because, you know how bad I want kids, yet you won't give me any."

"It's not that I don't want to, it's just we have the company to worry about."

"Jason, you don't make time for me like you use to. When I first met you, we couldn't keep our hands off of each other, now -" I sighed. "Now it seems like you're not attracted to me anymore."

"Aw' l babe. Naw' l, don't ever think that. I'm marrying you because no woman can satisfy me the way you do."

I blushed. "Prove it!" I called his bluff.

"Right here, right now?" He asked surprised.

"Yes, unless you're scared." I stood up and faced him, dropping down to my knees right in front of him. I pulled his zipper slowly as he stared into my eyes.

"Did you lock the door?" He asked as he took a deep breath.

Xtasy

I nodded as I pulled his beefy meat through his zipper. As I was about to put my mouth on his tootsie pop, he grabbed me by the face. "Let's skip the foreplay, and get down to business. You know sooner or later people will be knocking on the door." He leaned forward to taste my lips. His tongue found mine as he pulled me to my feet.

Jason's hands traveled up my long legs under my burgundy skirt to the thin string thong that hid between my ass cheeks. His dick was hard as it aimed at me from his lap. I felt his strong rough hands move my thong to the side, then he raised my skirt above my ass. His nose traveled down to my covered sex, he inhaled deeply, his eyes closed, and he smiled, satisfied.

Jason's strong fingers hooked the thin string that hid between my cum coated lips, he pulled my thong under my knees as I held onto his shoulder for support. Jason's meat stood up to attention as my pussy came into view. My pretty kitty was bald, except for the thin line of hair that I kept for a landing strip.

As Jason saw the landing strip, his eyes traveled up to mine. He'd always seen my kitty bald, it had been over a week since the last time we've been intimate, so this was like a little surprise.

Jason surprised me back as he gripped both of my cheeks, pulling my box to his mouth. I raised my right leg and positioned it on his chair, my sex lips slightly opened, giving his tongue game. People had always said the way to get a woman to do whatever you wanted was through her heart. That is somewhat true. But nothing locks me down better than a good orgasm. The way Jason was tongue kissing my pussy, I was close.

"Ohhh, Jason!" I moaned as I gripped his bald, smooth head. I had to catch myself from fucking his mouth like he does me when he's about to cum.

"Ohh, babe, ohh Godd-dd, don-don't stop!" Jason lapped at my center until I was bone dry, then I came, flooding his mouth with my sweet juices until it poured out the side of his mouth.

Jason stroked his meat until his hand was sticky with his own pre-cum. He pulled me over his lap, my wet, slippery box hovered over his meat. Jason eased me down slowly, my legs overlapping his. I felt his head pierce my center, my mouth opened, but no words came out.

Knock! Knock!

"Sir, you have an appointment here to see you!" Jason's secretary, Brandi yelled through the door.

I lifted myself up, but at the same time, Jason was pulling me down, trying to finish what we'd started.

"Ju-Just reschedule it!" Jason muttered as he placed his mushroom head at my opening. I grabbed his meat at the base. The thick vein ran down the side thumped under my touch, impatiently.

"It's Mr. Albertson, from Down South Killa records," Brandi said.

"Uhh!" Jason sighed. "Just, give me a minute!" Jason tried to pull me down on his lap, I slapped his hand and climbed over him.

"What, what you doing?" He asked as I grabbed my thong from the floor. I stepped into it and covered my sex.

"We can finish tonight, business first, remember," I said as I pulled my skirt down and smoothed it out. I reached in Jason's desk drawer and pulled out his febreze spray. I swished as I knew Jason was watching my every move, especially my ass. I sprayed the sweet-smelling fragrance around his office to cover up the sexual aroma that was evident in the air.

As I returned the fragrance to his desk, Jason stared at me with lust in his eyes. His dick was still in his hand, hard, but not as hard as before.

"So you're just going to leave me like this," he gestured to his exposed package.

I smirked. "I'll see you at home." I kissed his cheek and walked to the door. I unlocked it and looked over my shoulder, Jason stood up to fix himself. I opened the door, Brandi stood on the other side. As she noticed Jason fixing his clothes, she gave him a sour look that he didn't see.

I brushed past her and snickered as I did. The scandalous bitch thought I didn't see the way she was looking at Jason during the board meeting. At the meeting, Jason pretended to have an important call, and five minutes later, Brandi had to use the restroom. If 2+2 don't make 4, I'll pay you. They may have fooled everyone else in the meeting, but they didn't fool me. Then Jason's dick smelled like salty pussy. And what man in his right mind will pass up some head. Yeah, I know!

$$$

Chapter 10
-Cupid-

I sat on my director's chair as I watched my crew prepare for another film. The adult film awards was only a month away, and I had to be ready. Forget the Oscars, the AFA was the awards of the year for films. Last year Pandora's Poison won an award for 'Cumming from where I'm from'. Roman won a separate award for best performance. That one film put Pandora's Poison on the map. But if we don't continue to make hits, we will no longer be on the map; people will target us, and it'll feel like we fell from the face of the earth.

We were preparing to film a short sitcom, "Spank me now, cry later." It was only a six-episode sitcom, that I call a porn-com. I wasn't using Camilla, or Roman for the porn-com, even though they were my two best actors. I intended on using Nila, who was from India. Nila was made of pure beauty. Her skin was golden, smooth, and had a glow to it. She had legs like a run way model, and a bubble butt like a high dollar call girl. She had a bushy pussy that men drooled over. Her titties were the perfect size, and she wasn't afraid to make love to the camera.

Her partner for the porn-com was no other than Caesar Hawkins. Caesar was an actor that I had used before when I first started in the film industry. Back then, he was average. Over the years, he's taken performance classes, and he's much better.

Caesar is a favorite for a lot of women. I use Roman a lot because of his looks, but Caesar, when it comes to making people laugh, he's natural. A lot of women he's worked with always tell me how comfortable Caesar makes them.

Caesar is only five foot five, and light as a feather. But the women say he's packing a punch in his pants that knocks their pussy out. Caesar has wavy hair and wears a regular low-taper haircut. The one thing that stands out about Caesar is his eyes. His eyes are grey, like a wolf, and they're not contacts.

As I was looking at my crew setting the stage up, my attention was diverted as Karen and Amy walked into the room. I had been trying hard to dodge Karen after the sexual encounter we had in my office earlier. I could still smell her scent on me, and it smelled good. I had told Karen to give Amy a tour, forgetting she would have to bring Amy here.

Karen looked at me and blushed. She couldn't hide the secret that I was trying hard to bury. Amy followed her eyes and gave me an innocent smile of her own. I wondered if Amy was able to put two and two together. Who was I kidding, I knew Amy could smell the sex that escaped from my office as I opened the door. Oh well.

Karen walked up to me with Amy on her left side. "And this is the last screening room, where mostly two or three stages are set up at a time," Karen said to Amy, yet she looked at me as she said it.

"So Amy," I said. "How'd you like the tour?"

"It was useful. This place is hugely larger than it appears from the outside. Karen was a huge help, she informed me of your routine. And I took notes and stored a lot of them in my head. I don't know how I'll be able to replace Karen shoes she's aid out before me, but I'll do everything to try."

Karen smiled at the compliment Amy gave her. Amy was right, Karen was good at what she did, and without a doubt, she left big shoes to fill, or should I say, heels.

"So, with everything she showed you, do you still want to work here?" I asked Amy.

She nodded. "It's different from what I'm used to, but yes, I do."

"You haven't really seen much. I don't want you to go home and complain to Ced' when you see naked men walk past you like it's nothing. Or you have to sit in on a scene of a man having sex with a woman."

She shook her head. "I'ma grown woman. Naked men have never scared me before, and they never will."

I nodded as Karen stared at me. Karen looked at the bulge between my legs as if she had x-ray vision. I ruined her to the point she would never be the same.

Moan in my Mouth

"Karen, do me a favor, call Caesar and tell him we're going to cancel today's session until tomorrow, I've already talked to Nala. She knows."

Karen nodded and walked off. As she walked away, she looked over her shoulder at me. I hate that I had to just throw away some amazing pussy, but Karen was making our encounter too obvious. Damn, God, and the way He made a woman's insides feel so damn good.

"Amy, take a seat," I said pointing to the chair beside me. Amy took her seat, her skirt rose a little, and tightened around her thick thighs. I had never witnessed an Asian as thick as her. It made me wonder if her ass was the reason Cedrick was marrying her. She was beautiful as hell too, but her ass was heaven. Sacred, and to be worshiped. She had a body that was made for a camera.

"I know you're my best friend's fiance, so you're expecting me to show you favoritism. I'm fairly hard on my workers, for specific reasons. At the moment, we're making two films, and a porn-com to compete for the adult film awards. This place will get a little hectic, and most nights, we'll be working late to finish up the projects. If you're not up to the task, it's okay to let me know."

Amy smiled a very beautiful smile, her teeth were white like she had them bleached. "Cupid, I'm here to work, I'm not asking for special privileges. If we have to work from sun up, to sundown, I'll be here. Whatever you need me to do, I'll make sure it gets done."

As she spoke, I could do nothing but nodded my head. Her beauty was captivating. Amy stood up and smoother her skirt down.

"I'll be back, I know you prefer blueberry muffins, but only the tops. Bottled water, with lemon slices." I nodded, Karen had taught her well.

As she started to walk off, she stopped and faced me." Cupid, it's not going to be easy to get rid of me. Especially when I like the vibe that's here. So, relax." She showed me that beautiful smile that caused me to nod and stare. This was all Ced's fault, and I hoped he knew it.

Xtasy

***

-Cedrick-

I looked around my office to make sure everything was as it should. I had a sit-in to hear a few tracks on the radio station, 97.9 The Beat in Dallas. I had heard of the new up-and-coming sensation known as Zig Zag, now I had the chance to manage his music.

"Oh, Cedrick, where you headed off somewhere?" Trineka asked as she stood in front of my office door.

"I was headed off to listen in on Zig Zag's radio sit-in." I looked at her long legs. Back in my younger days, I would've climbed them without the fear of falling. I was a changed man now. An engaged man at that.

"Oh, I was trying to see if you still wanted to grab that coffee, but I'll let you get back to what you do best."

She started to walk away, but I stopped her. "Trineka, wait." She faced me, her freckles matched her skin effectively. "I could use some company, that's if you don't mind?" Trineka smiled. "Of course, I could use some fresh air. Let me get my purse, and I'll meet you-"

"We'll use my car," I said.

She smiled again. "I'll see you at your parking spot."

***

I sat in my G-Wagon, I was glad that I went to the detail shop the day before. Bit Lue's made my truck look like I'd just drove it off the lot. I had to be sure to tip Javier the next time I went by the shop, even though he barely understood a word I said.

The passenger door opened, Trineka stepped into the G-Wagon, her strawberry scent mixed well with the fresh car smell. She closed the door and sat her purse on the floor. "So, did you tell

Moan in my Mouth

your fiance where you were going?" I asked as I drove out of the parking lot.

"Nope. Until I say I do, I'ma do as I please. Did you tell your fiance who you were with?" She countered.

I shook my head. "No, she trusts me."

"As she should," she said.

"Normally, I would let artists do their radio interviews alone, but Zig Zag will be doing this at a studio, and it will be streamed on Facebook and Instagram live."

She nodded. "That's why Jason hired you, you do things differently, which is good. Most artists think that the owners skim them millions, without doing any real work. You showing up to the interview will prove different, which is great."

I smiled, "us,"

She looked at me. "What do you mean?"

"It's not just me showing up, it's us. We're a team. Bloody Lyrics is the brand."

Trineka smiled again, then her smile faded. "You know, Jason asked about you earlier."

"Oh really. What did you say?"

"I told him, basically, that you're the right man for the job. That you're a smart investment, but nothing changes overnight. For God's sake, you just started."

"What if I'm not the man for the job though?"

"But you are." She said.

"How would you honestly know?" I asked. "You just met me." Maybe Jason was right, I thought to myself. I had a lot of success on the west coast, but this was the south, and it was a lot of competition in the south.

"I know because I saw the confidence in your walk when you walked through the door. I know I just met you, but I can, haven't you seen it firsthand when I gave you the artists' files.?"

She made a valid point. "But, what if I fail still?" I asked her as I looked at her.

"Then we've failed!"

73

Xtasy

***

We pulled up to superb sounds, a recording studio in north Dallas that Zig Zag frequently used. The interview with 97.9 The Beat was to take place at the studio. I parked and opened Trineka's door, it was a forced habit as a gentleman.

We walked inside, I had to show my Bloody Lyrics badge to be able to enter the session. The on-air sign was bright red. We were led in and ushered to the back where a few other spectators listened in. Trineka pulled out her iPhone and recorded the interview.

I looked at the artist known as Zig Zag. He had blown up in the game. He was much like Franko Zay, they were both crips and ex-cons. Zig Zag was just a different race; he was a mixed breed, Mexican and White. There was a lot of controversy behind Zig Zag. No doubt he put on for his city, Austin, and he ripped the north side with pride. The controversy came from him being an Insane Gangsta Crip. But Zig Zag had promised his fans this interview to clear the smoke.

97.9 - "Let's cut all the bullshit Zig Zag. Why do you feel like you deserve to be the next big thing to come out of Texas?"

ZigZag - "I don't feel like I deserve shit. When you start thinkin' like that, yo start to develop a sense of entitlement, and that way of thinkin' causes you to let up off the gas."

97.9 - "That kinda goes against the disposition of most rappers. When we talk to artists, a lot of y'all feel like y'all have earned the top spot."

Zig Zag - "I'm not most rappers."

97.9 - "What separates you then?"

Zig Zag - "Hunger. Work ethic, perception."

97.9 - "Talk to us about where you're from. How did you come up?"

Zig Zag - "I'm still on the come up. No matter how much I elevate, meaning, there's nothing special that goes on in my hood that doesn't go on in every other hood in America. Shottas and

Moan in my Mouth

gorillas tryna push a jag! Dogs turning into snakes. Rats taking down wolves."
97.9 - "Jungle shit." He laughed.
Zig Zag - "Know'n saying."
97.9 - "So, let's address the elephant in the room. Why do you, someone who's not black, feel like you should be accepted into black culture?"
Zig Zag - "I'm not looking for acceptance."
97.9 - "But hip-hop is our culture. You have to be able to acknowledge that. Given your ethnicity, you're an outsider."
Zig Zag - "Can you define ethnicity for me? What makes up an ethnic group?"
97.9 - "Well, I can sum it up for you. Basically, it's-"
Zig Zag - "Large groups of people classed according to common traits and customs."
97.9 - "Well yeah, so-"
Zig Zag - "A member of a minority ethnic group who retains its customs, language, or social views."
97.9 - "Exactly. You're not black."
Zig Zag - "Obviously. But, if you feel like skin color brings you closer to somebody than a mind frame, way of life or morals and virtues can, then I don't know why I'm even talking to you. I wouldn't want to be associated with you."
97.9 - "That is a really good point, and I couldn't agree with you more. But, you know, that there are people out there that sees shit differently."
Zig Zag - "Again, I'm not looking for acceptance. I am who I am, and who I'm not, I'll never be."
97.9 - "Are you concerned that people won't take your music serious because of this? Like you might get overlooked."
Zig Zag - "I ain't no emotional nigga, cuz. From an occupational standpoint, of course, I want you to listen to me cuz, that means I'm gettin' paid. But, as a man, I have a strong sense of identity. I won't change how I am because your mind is too narrow for me to navigate through it. I'ma just go over some people's head, and I'm cool with that."

97.9 - "Real Shit!"

Zig Zag - "For the record though, I just spent the last decade of my life in prison, from the age of seventeen to twenty-seven. The penitentiary itself is probably the most racist place in America. You're supposed to ride with 'your people, 'your race'."

97.9 - "What did you do?"

Zig Zag - "I gotta blue bandana tattooed on my chest, I'm crippin'!"

97.9 - "How did that affect you?"

Zig Zag - "That's who looked out for me, and vice versa. The white boys and the Mexicans tend to clique up together against the blacks. I ain't gotta tell you that the incarceration rate or black people is higher than any other race, so they're going to try and gain control."

97.9 - "So, what's your point?"

Zig Zag - "My point is, I think for, and with the black community. I was raised in jail, cuz. That's where I grew up, and where I developed."

97.9 - "Inside the black community."

Zig Zag - "For what it's worth."

97.9 - "So you got yo, 'black card'?" he laughed.

Zig Zag - "Oh God!" Zig Zag laughed too.

97.9 - "Well, you invited us to your studio session for a reason. You ready to spit some of that hot shit?"

Zig Zag - "Overstood."

97.9 - "Before you do that, thank you for the interview, I appreciate your time and what you have to offer for the culture."

Zig Zag - " Likewise."

$$$

Chapter 11
-Zig Zag-

I was glad the interview was over. I wasn't afraid to speak my mind, so the questions didn't bother me. I knew a lot of people had questions about me, and what I represented. I never shy'd away from the questions, and I never bit my tongue for no nigga. I was who I am because it's who I am. I talked the way I talked because it's the way I talk. I was glad the interview was over because no matter what I said in interviews, niggas were gon' still hate. The only thing that no one complained about was my music.

I walked into the booth and took my designer frames off. I pulled my hoodie over my head that had the words, 'saneless - society' written across it in bold letters. I smoothed out my shirt that had my logo dripping off the front of it. I then took that shirt off, only to be standing in the booth with a different shirt on. A more permanent one. My entire life was displayed on my body, from my gang affiliation to the Insane Gangsta crips, to family portraits that would forever be displayed on my body.

I passed my clothes to the only person that came to the 'yo with me. She was a visual checklist of what a bad bitch is supposed to be. The type of bitch that a nigga is supposed to bag when he blows up. Only thing is, she was there before the fame, before the money, during the struggle.

I stood in the soundproof booth, spectators watching me like their favorite TV show. I stood before them looking like a contradiction: Boyish good looks, with the pain and struggle of a grown man refusing to be ignored. No jewelry on, but vibe screamin' money. Niggas prayed to be in the position I was in, yet I still had to prove myself as I stood behind the mic with the aura of a vet.

The beat that I bought by Metro Boomin' drops. The beat had an infectious rhythm of trap meets the band camp with a baseline that could only be found in the south. I dropped some jewels over the beat, both cappin and super crackin'.

Xtasy

"Yeah ... shoutout to the hata's this finna create ... and the ones already in existence ... from the nowf side to yo' side. This shit ain't happen overnight ... best advice I can give anyone strugglin' out there, just respect the process, and hopefully the pressure you're facin' makes diamonds, instead of bust pipes, know what I'm sayin' ... royal!"

"Somebody said real niggas was extinct/What type of shit is that?
If that's the case/then I'ma livin' breathin' walkin' artifact.
Everybody in my face/tryna give me dap
Music give me hope/and I'm just tryna give that back
Some people see my skin tone/I know that shit confuse 'em
Especially when I'm on the eat/smootha than a hoova
Judge me if you wanna miss out if you choose to
I'm somewhere gettin' money, just in case a nigga lose ya"
I let the beat ride before I started talkin' shit again.
I knew I had everybody in the room with goosebumps, but I still felt like they weren't convinced.
"Yeah ... what's all the staring fo'?" I asked to all the spectators outside the booth going dumb, begging me to keep going.
So I gave in.
"Before I start, I need to let some shit be known off the rip.
O.T.G originator/Insane Gangsta Crip
Nawf side where I reside/Austin Texas full of pride
It's tattooed multiple times, look at me I will remind
As humble as they come, ain't got no chip on my shoulda
And I'm straight up out the slums/so my language kinda vulgar
Shawty if I call you bitch/it wasn't meant to offend you
And I say the word 'nigga', quite a lot, plain an simple
I ain't putin' on no act/I'm just putin' on, and that's facts
A lot of bitches in my hotel room/ and I put 'em all on they back
Couple niggas with me since grade school/I put 'em all in my camp

Moan in my Mouth

Get som' real niggas while locked up/my Jpay full of stamps
And my mama drive something brand new/my dad do and my bitch too
Baby mama ain't gotta worry bout nothin/despite what we been through
Our kids straight, and her kid too/plus anybody I'm kin to
Much love in my neighborhood/but I'm still strapped when I flip through"
The beat slowed so I could talk my shit. "Yeah ... cuz ain't no
Tellin' ... what the next nigga thinkin'. I'ma do whatever I gotta ...
To make sure I'm still breathin'. Cuz I'm the breadwinner ... And
they dependin' on me ... I gotta get it for 'em. Yeah!"
"Insane on my fade/Rundberg on my shoulder blades
This lifestyle I live is lavish/but the background story ain't
Thank God when I'm wakin up/roll it up, then take a puff
Baby know that our pockets right/cuz I don't go to sleep if we don't make
Enough
Where I'm from they label us/love to sticky situation us
Thumb tackin' and staple us/anything to disable us
From lasabers to mercedes trucks/settin' trends with amazon' looks
Don't let designer shoes call yo' bluff/nigga started out lacin' chucks
Nigga, started out loadin clips, makin flips on stolen zips
Fo deep in a stolen whip/only one ain't smokin' dip
Born an' raised in the guttah/two brothers sister and mother
Step dad puchin' her/but i know that he loved her
Lookin' up to my cousin/but cocaine got him buggin'
Them good grades don't cut it, when that refrigerator got nothin'
So fuck school we thuggin'/mind on runnin' them bands up
But them graduates got jobs now and all I got was handcuffed
...

Xtasy

… but this the life we chose … the only life we know … we Gotta want better for ourselves … that's why I'm doin' me!"

I opened my eyes as the beat stopped. I couldn't figure out when I had closed them. The spectators outside the booth cheered and applauded me, yet I couldn't hear through the thick walls. My bitch showed me her phone, Instagram Live was showing, yet all I noticed was the half a million viewers that had just watched me let my nuts hang.

My bitch kissed me on the lips, I sucked on her bottom lip as she pulled away. Wasn't shit like a down, bad bitch that's a certified rider. That's why she went where I went, cause when I was on lock, she did the time with me, day for day. Lawyers and the commissary ain't gon' pay itself.

$$$

Chapter 12
-Cedrick-

I raced into the house after seeing Amy's Porsche wasn't in the driveway. I had a great day at work today. The live interview with Zig Zag went great. He raked in a half a million views, and he made me proud with the way he handled himself. It wouldn't be long before Zig Zag was the hottest thing to come out of Texas.

Before coming home, I stopped by the grocery store to get something to cook for dinner. Amy had texted me and said that she would be coming home late. I was just glad that she had a job, she always complained about how bored she was at home by herself.

I sat the grocery bags on the kitchen counter, took my suit jacket off and laid it on the barstool. I washed my hands clean and sat the pink salmon in the sink to thaw out. I grabbed the salad mix and tossed it into a strainer to rinse. I wanted to take the load off of Amy and surprise her with dinner, so I decided to take up the role of cooking for tonight.

As I preheated the stove, I ran off to our bedroom to prepare Amy a bubble bath. The jacuzzi-size tub was chosen by Amy for nights like this, meaning it was big enough for both of us. I filled the tub up, then turned the heat on, and the jets to keep the bubbles afloat. A smile appeared on my face, it was about to be a great day altogether.

***

-Amy-

Today wasn't as bad as I thought it would be. After Karen finally warmed up to me, she showed me how to organize Cupid's schedule and his office. As I was organizing Cupid's office, I found a woman's thong in his restroom, as Karen noticed it in my hand, she snatched it up and blushed. I had already figured something was going on between them two, the thong explained

Xtasy

why she was acting towards me in the beginning. The only thing I was off about, was the person, OG. The whole day at work, I kept waiting to hear whose name was O, but it never came back up.

I turned my key in the lock as I opened the door. I could smell dinner in the air, and it smelled like fish and shrimp. I sat my purse on the side table and followed my nose to the kitchen. To my amazement, Cedrick stood in the kitchen in an apron and nothing underneath. I laughed, causing him to face me.

"Hey beautiful, how was your first day at work?" Ced asked as he kissed me softly on the lips.

"It was different," I said as I watched his bare ass as he walked back to the skillet.

"So you didn't like it?" He asked.

"No, I did. I just had to get used to the constant movement. Cupid often thought of plots and scenes that he wanted jotted down, and he had a lot of ideas."

Ced' laughed. "Glad you liked it. I got something else you're going to like." He said as he turned the stove off. He grabbed my hand and led me to the bathroom.

"What about the food?" I asked

"Bathe first, then we'll eat. Fair?"

I smiled as I saw the bathtub water vibrating, bubbles popped up all around. I looked to Ced' he untied the apron as it fell to the floor, his body looked toned and hard. He pressed play on my apple speaker, my favorite song by John Legend began to play.

"This," he said as he handed me a wine glass filled with white wine. "Is to a happy, loving, sexual marriage." He smiled as we clinked our wine glasses together. We both took a nice size sip from our glasses. Cedrick sat his glass down and stepped behind me.

"You're going to be the perfect husband."

He laughed. "I'ma start by being the perfect fiance." He unzipped my shirt, I slightly crossed my legs so that he could pull it down. As my skirt hit the floor, I stepped out of it.

Moan in my Mouth

Cedrick pulled me into his embrace from the back. His dick rubbed against my backside. He held me as we let our bodies sway in sync with John Legends' harmonic voice.

"... And you say that you're not worth it
And get hung up on your flaws
But in my eyes you are perfect
As your are
As your are
... I will never try to change you, change you
I will always want the same you, same you
Swear on everything I pray to
That I won't break your heart,"

Cedrick trailed kisses down my neck. If he could taste the workday of salty sweat, he didn't let it show. As he kissed my neck, his hands moved inside the thin fabric that covered my sex. He eased his finger under the thin material and hooked my thong sliding it down with ease.

"First, we bathe, then, we eat." He said as he guided me into the hot water.

The water was hot as I stepped inside. My muscles relaxed under the vibrating water. Cedrick stepped inside, he sat down facing me. We had purchased the jacuzzi tub specifically for moments like this.

I stood in front of him, my kitty was only inches from his face. He showed a lot of discipline as he washed my legs first, then he made his way down to my feet. I held onto his shoulder as he did. I looked at him as he cleaned my body with expertise.

Although I commended him for his discipline, my kitty was purring, anxious for him to touch it. "Turn," he said calmly.

I faced the wall, Cedrick stood up behind me, the heat between my legs was hotter than the jacuzzi water. Cedrick washed my shoulder blades, then washed down to my back. As he kissed my left shoulder, a chill shot through my body out of nowhere.

"Open your legs," he demanded.

I opened my legs, the anticipation was killing me silently. The only thing that could be heard was the vibration from the tub and my beating heart. John Legend even stopped singing for the action.

The soft, fluffy sponge moved between my legs, as the sponge brushed my wet sex lips, my legs damn near gave out. I placed my hand on the wall in front of me, it was the only thing that could help at the moment. Lord knows he's against what'll happen next.

Cedrick worked the sponge between my sex lips, then he worked it between my ass cheeks lingering there for a moment longer. I didn't feel when the sponge hit the water, but I felt Ced's strong fingers slip inside of me, two to be exact.

"Ced', yes!" I moaned as he finally began to relieve the anticipation that had built up.

"You like that?" I nodded with no words. "You know I love you, right?"

I nodded again as he plucked my clit back and forth like a guitar string. "Do you love me back?"

I nodded again. For some reason, I couldn't find out where I misplaced my tongue. Cedrick's fingers moved faster over my swollen clit, my head fell forward, I had to place my other hand on the wall for better support.

"Say you love me," Ced said as he gripped my ass, pulling them apart as he sunk down in the water, striking my clit with his tongue.

The words I wanted to say came out as a bunch of mumbling. I looked over my shoulder, nothing made sense to me at the moment; life went as a blur as Ced's dick spread my walls like Moses did at the red sea. I held on to the wall like my life depended on it.

"Oh, God, babe-eee!" My words came back all at once. I shook my head in bliss as Ced dug into my pussy like his favorite dish.

"That's right babe, tell daddy how good it feels, huh," he said as he held onto my shoulders and Jackhammered my kitty.

"It feels, so-ooo, good, dad-dee!" I felt my kitty grip his dick, and my cum thickened around his dick.

Moan in my Mouth

Cedrick pulled out and laid down in the jacuzzi tub. My legs felt like jello, he grabbed my hand and pulled me down on his lap. I positioned his dick at my opening, as he filled me up, his mouth opened. We moved together perfectly as water eased over the sides of the tub. I loved the man that made me cum at will. I loved my life and everything in it. And I couldn't wait to spend the rest of it as Mrs. Amy Montgomery.

$$$

Xtasy

Chapter 13
-Cupid-

The week went by fast. Work was as work has always been. Exciting, yet stressful. People feel that I shouldn't be able to complain about my job. I get to record people having sex over and over, so people think it's super easy. It's not! For one, it's hard to concentrate when you're watching a woman you think is beautiful get spanked naked. It takes a lot of self-control to master the art of not getting a hard-on during filming. God knows how OG has a mind of his own.

What made work so stressful this week was the fact that Karen wouldn't be coming back. Even though she had a full week left of her two-weeks notice, she and I decided it was best for her to not come the following week. It was beginning to get hard for me to keep my hands off of her. Every chance we got, we fucked. I had to get rid of her, fast. I just had to. For my own good, and OG's.

Amy picked up where Karen left off. Not in that way, get your mind out of the gutter. I'm talking about work-wise. Amy was a great secretary. She beat me to work every day, and as soon as I walked into the building, she would hand me my favorite coffee, and take my jacket. I often wondered if she welcomed Cedrick at the front door like she did me. Our conversations were always about work, only because I didn't trust my own mind sometimes.

It was Friday again. Cedrick wanted to have another guy's night in his man cave. I talked him out of it and talked him into going out with me. Nemo's wife wouldn't let him out of the house, which is the prime example why I would never get married. Uncle Sam somehow got out of the house. He probably waited until his wife 'Shonda fell asleep first.

I rented a Mercedes Sprinter van to accompany us for the night, that way, we would all be able to get drunk and enjoy the night. When I told the fellas that we were going to the Mavericks

Xtasy

versus the Lakers game, they were in awe, especially being that I got us floor seats.

"You can practically smell the wave grease on Lebron's hair; we're so close." Uncle Sam joked.

Our seats were on the opposite side of the teams' benches. We sat across from the Lakers bench. The arena was sold out, the only thing is that Luka wasn't playing, so it would be an easy win for Lebron and the Lakers. Inside the van, I had downed a couple of shots of Patron, so I was already feeling myself. We ordered a few cups of beer, Cedrick ordered him a small order of wings.

"So, have my wife been behaving herself?" Ced asked as he offered me a wing.

"Why wouldn't she. I told you, we're-"

"A professional industry," Ced said, cutting me off. "I know I didn't mean it like that. What I meant was, has she been working hard?"

"You should know me well by now, when it comes to business, I make sure I take care of it. Haven't you noticed that our wife comes home late every night?" I laughed at my own joke.

Ced laughed and said. "I've noticed. Thankfully you haven't satisfied her, because she comes home sexually aroused." Ced laughed again.

Cedrick and I always joked around. He knew I would never have sex with his fiance, no matter how beautifully sculptured she was. Although I did have a wet dream the other night about her, and it was Xtreme. Oh God fell in love at first sight. She had satisfied him fully. She even did what other women couldn't. She swallowed him whole, all the way down to his twin brothers. It was the most amazing feeling I've ever felt. Then, I woke up. And I haven't been able to get her out of my mind since. It is hard to walk by her every day, let alone smell her sweet scent when she walks by me.

"So, how's work coming along for you? I asked. Uncle Sam jumped up as Carmelo made a three-pointer.

"I've made a little progress, I've been helping Belofante get ready to put out some new music. We'll start on that Monday.

Moan in my Mouth

"I thought he had given up on music, I hadn't heard one of his songs in a while."

Ced shook his head as he bit into another wing. "He's doing the family thing, so he took some time off, but he's back, and I'ma make the audience remember why they always loved him."

As I was about to say something, a young kid sat beside me. He had to be at least nine, or ten years old. He was light-skinned, like he was mixed. A Caucasian woman sat beside him. She looked of relation to him, like they shared the same nose and chin, yet she looked too young to be his mother.

I laughed at the little kid as I looked at the Kansas City Chiefs jersey that he had on. It was a Patrick Mahomes jersey. "Kid, you're in the wrong stadium, aren't you?" I teased him.

The little kid looked up at me, his haircut was like Mahomes too. Patrick Mahomes had won over all the light-skinned kids with good, as all the dark-skinned kids pretended to be Lamar Jackson.

"You're talking 'bout my jersey." The kid said. The dirty blonde-haired woman that sat beside him looked over at me.

"I guess you can say that. You do know that this is a basketball game and not a football game."

The kid nodded. "I'm wearing it so the world can see who's going to the Super Bowl yet again."

"You really think they're going to the Super Bowl again? Why?" I asked.

"Because there's nothing like having fans and then losing them only cause we lost the Super Bowl, then started the season off bad. P-Mack wants to show them who's boss."

"P-Mack?" I asked.

"Yes, I call Mahomes P-Mack."

I laughed at the kid. "Do you know anything about basketball?"

He nodded. "I do, you want to make a bet on this game?"

I looked at the kid in shock, he called me out. His babysitter popped him on the back of the head. "Tristian, what did I tell you about trying to gamble."

"Come on ma' not in public," Tristan complained. I looked at his mother. I mean really looked at her. Her beauty met my eye.

"It's okay, Ms. He's actually more fun talking to than my own friends." I looked over my shoulders to Cedrick and Sam, they were both into the game.

"My name is Cupid." I shook the kid's hand, then his mother's. "Nice to meet you, Tristan." Tristan let my hand go as he looked at my watch.

"Is that a real Rolex?" He asked.

I laughed and held my arm out to him. "Listen and see."

Tristan placed his ear to my Rolex and listened. "Wow, I can't hear nothing. It's really true ma', real Rolex don't tick, tock."

His mother laughed. Her teeth were perfect. Straight, and white as hell. I couldn't help but wonder how old she was. She had already won ten points with me seeing that her kid was well dressed, and he had a black father. I looked at her ring finger, not that it really mattered. If a woman wanted to cheat on her husband, then that was his problem, not mine. But, she didn't have a ring on, which would make the chase that much easier.

"So, about that bet," I said as I pulled two five-dollar bills from my money clip. "Who you're taking?" I asked.

"You do know Luka's not playing."

He nodded. "You might as well say Anthony Davis isn't playing either, he hasn't made a shot all night." I laughed, he was right, A-D hadn't made a single shot. It was the Lebron show. Even though Luka wasn't playing, the Mavericks were keeping up.

"My ten dollars, against," I looked at his mom as she watched us interact. "My ten dollars against your mom's phone number." I looked at her and smiled. She blushed and looked at Tristian.

"Deal," he held his hand out to shake on it.

"Really Tristian. My number, for only ten dollars." She smiled.

"Don't worry ma', I'll give you five dollars once we win." The kid was funny, I couldn't help but laugh.

Moan in my Mouth

I looked at the court, Lebron fed Anthony Davis a nice pass, Anthony Davis pulled up for the fade-away and made the shot. I looked at Tristian and smiled. All he could do was shake his head.

***

"I told you! I told you!" Tristan jumped up from his seat as The unicorn made another 3-pointer, tying the game up.

I couldn't do anything but shake my head now. It wasn't that I was about to lose my ten dollars, it was more so that I was about to miss out on the opportunity at getting Tristians sexy mom's number.

Lebron did what he always did, which was perform. He made a pull-up three from the Mavericks logo, no exaggeration. I looked over at Tristian who had a huge smile on his face, even though he was impressed. The rest of the game ended up being a shoot-out, but the Lakers won by three as their rookie who they nicknamed A-R 15 made the game-winning shot.

I had to hold my smile in, just in case little Tristian was a sore loser. I shook his hand and said. "They fought hard. If they would've had Luka, they might've won."

"Yeah, you could be right," he said, then looked towards his mom.

"I can't believe you gambled me off like that." She said as she handed me her phone. "Put your number in here," I took her phone and programmed my number, saving it under "Cupid-NBA." As I began to hand her my phone, she looked at me and shook her head. "You really hustled my son, so I'm not going to give you my number until I decide to call you."

I couldn't help but smile. "Can I at least get your name?"

She stood up as the crowd began to clear out. "Brianna."

"Brianna," I said out loud for my memory. "Tristian, nice doing business with you." I shook his hand again.

"She's never going to call you," Tristan said.

I laughed. "You wanna bet?"

Xtasy

Brianna smiled. "Come on Tristian, you've had your share of gambling for today."

I winked at Brianna as she and Tristian walked away. I shook my head as I watched her in her jeans. I prayed she called, I know OG felt the same.

"Look back, please look back," I whispered to myself as I watched them walking farther and farther. To my amazement, she looked back at me and smiled. Yeah, she would definitely call.

$$$

Chapter 14
-Amy-

I woke up last night to Cedrick crawling in our bed. He was drunk, I smelled it all over his breath. I stripped him out of his clothes. His dick was hard, so I gave him some mind-blowing head that I knew he wouldn't remember the next day, then I tossed a sheet over him.

When I woke up, I cooked breakfast for Ced and me. As I was carrying Ced's plate to him, I heard a noise from Ced's mancave. I eased down the steps to investigate. As I made it downstairs, I saw Cupid sprawled out on the futon snoring. The blanket was on the floor. He had no shirt on, his jeans were on the floor. The next thing that caught my eye was his penis.

"Oh my fuckin', God!" I said a little too loud, then tried to cover my mouth to prevent any more outbursts. Cupid was completely naked, well, he had his socks still on. He had what men called, 'morning wood', except his was more of a log. It was weird, like his dick was staring at me like it could sense I was in the room.

I slowly backed up the stairs, I didn't want Cupid to catch me while he was naked. Me seeing him naked wasn't a problem. The problem would be, him seeing me see him naked. Now that would make it weird at work. As I made it to the top of the stairs, I took another peep downstairs to get another glimpse of his dick, it was the biggest I've ever seen.

I shook my head, 'you're engaged to his best friend'. I reminded myself.

"Is he still sleeping?" Ced asked, startling me as he walked up beside me.

"Uh-h, ye-es, he's still asleep." I was hoping Cedrick wouldn't go downstairs, and he did.

"I'ma wake him up, we have a lot to do today," Ced said as he began to walk down the stairs.

"Ced, wait!" Ced stopped and looked at me. "Your food, it'll get cold. You know how you hate cold eggs."

Xtasy

"I'll be right up," Ced said as he walked down the stairs. I was on his tail like a drunk driver.

"You're up, Amy said you were asleep," Ced said as he shook hands with Cupid.

I looked at Cupid with my hands on my hips. He stood before us fully dressed, looking as if ten seconds ago he wasn't just stark naked.

"Nah, I knew we had a lot to do, so I got up and got prepared. You know I can drink a case of beers and still be up before the rooster croaks."

"Good. Let's eat, Amy cooked breakfast, then we can go tux shopping."

I looked at Cupid, I was at loss for words. I mean, I had just seen him naked, now he was fully dressed. I know I wasn't imagining him naked. Or was I? No, I know what I saw. His monster penis was there, staring at me, overlapping his balls, protecting them like a security guard. I know what I saw. His dick would forever leave a stain on my brain. But, how did he get dressed so fast? Did he hear us coming back down the stairs? That would only mean he was already woke. If he was already awake, that would mean he saw me. And if he saw me, then he saw me looking, no, staring at his monster penis log.

I looked at Cupid, my eyes traveled to the land of the forbidden, a place no engaged woman should venture. Yet I couldn't help myself. I had to make sure I saw what I know I saw. I looked at his jeans, imagining I could see through them, salutary vision. The outline, the print, it traveled to his thigh. I tried to look harder, to see the head, that would surely confirm everything. Like a police lineup, a face I"ll never forget.

I looked, stared at his print. Something in his pants jumped, flinched. I jumped back, my hand went to my mouth to hold my gasp in. I looked at Cupid, he smiled, then winked. I knew right then that I was in trouble.

***

Moan in my Mouth

-Cupid-

After I and Ced went tux shopping, he dropped me off at home. He invited me back over to his house to watch some games, but I declined the offer. Not that I had anything to do, I just had to decline. I didn't want to put too much on Amy's mind, I had already hit her with the sneak peek.

This morning, when Amy saw me naked, I saw her. In fact, I knew she was coming. I saw her cooking, and I knew Ced was passed out drunk. I made a loud noise just so she could come downstairs. I didn't have to stroke OG to get him to rise, he was like yeast, as soon as he felt heat, he rose on his own.

Amy stared at OG, barely blinking. At first, I thought she could scream, or run upstairs, but she didn't. She stared, captivated, brainwashed by OG, stuck, without a second thought of who I was. Why did I do it? Because it's the dog in me. The freak in me. Hell, the man in me. I did it just like all men measure their penis, just to see the outcome. Just to know. It doesn't mean I'm perverted; it just means I was right. The bigger dick always wins.

I could see the look in Amy's eyes, the lust, the fire. Sin was in her mind, isn't that where it all starts. She wanted to touch it, to hold it, cut it off and take it with her, to sew it on Ced so she could have the best of both worlds. I almost let out a laugh as she began to walk up the stairs until she came back for another look. That's when I knew Ced had a freak on his hands.

Then she came back with Ced, I had already dressed. The look on her face, God, it was priceless. She didn't know what to do. I kept it playa; I held a straight face. She shocked me though. She did the unthinkable. She went into a daze, hypnotized, stuck on my junk. If she had seen through vision, I knew she would've counted my pubic hairs. I showed her who's the boss though. I had practiced the trick since I was a kid. When I was younger, I would tie a string to OG, and tie a carrot to the other end. I would use all my strength to lift the carrot with only my dick muscle. Over the years, I would replace the carrot with something a little heavier,

Xtasy

like a marble. Now, I can make OG stand up at will. It's my favorite party trick.

I felt bad as Ced told me how much he loved her. How he couldn't wait to spend the rest of his life with her. It saddens me. I just didn't understand it. I didn't understand men. I had to be the greatest man alive, the smartest. I mean, the bible showed us about women. Eve, the prime example. Conniving, sneaky, and untrustworthy. I'm not a preacher, and I can't quote more than John 3:16. But I do remember coming across a passage where God said you couldn't find one good woman. Now, if I don't know anything else, I know God can't lie! So what does that tell you? Trust no woman.

Men, when they finally decide to pop the question, they should first ask the question, 'Are you a freak?' If they're afraid to ask, they should put her through the test. It's simple and easy. Whenever you're about to get intimate, let her pick a porno to play. If she looks up, 'BBC' which is (Big Black Cock), and you know yours is small or average, then you're in trouble, She's not the one. Another way to find out is to take her to a sex store; let her pick out a dildo. Now, if she's with you, she'll be generous, and pick one that resembles yours, just to spare your feelings. But, if you let her go by herself make sure to check her bag when she comes back. Don't be surprised if Mandingo is tucked inside. The easiest way to find out is to challenge yourself. Try peeing in on your knees. If you still pee on the seat, you're in big, big trouble.

$$$

Chapter 15
-Cedrick-

I accomplished a lot this past weekend. Cupid and I went shopping for our tuxes. I got fitted for mine, Cupid decided to wait, saying he'll gain a lot of weight before the wedding. Everything else was left up to Amy. The only thing left I had to do was go ring shopping. I was saving that for last. I couldn't do that with Cupid, he didn't believe in marriage like that. I needed a woman's perspective, so I decided to ask Trineka when the time came.

I felt I would have a great week seeing how great my weekend went. I had to get Belofante in the studio; that was at the top of my list, then check in with the rest of the artists.

I stepped out of my office, Trineka was already heading my way as if she could read my mind. I smiled, as did she. She flowed; like someone was carrying her. I noticed how beautiful she actually was. Her smile, her long puffy hair, her perfect height, her long shinny toned legs. The freckles that blessed her smooth skin. I couldn't help but think of how lucky Jason was. He had a beauty. A barbie. I wondered if she liked it rough, most good girls did. Amy sure did.

"Mr. Montgomery, you're all smiles today," Trineka said, putting me on blast.

If she hadn't said anything, my jaws would've eventually started hurting how hard I was smiling. "It's going to be a great week this week," I said playing it off.

"Oh, fill me in."

"Belofante's getting back in the studio," She nodded.

"Drill is going to drop a new song. Franko's going to be on The Breakfast Club. Bloody Lyrics will get a lot of publicity for that. And, seeing how many views Zig Zag got for his live studio recording, I thought that we should make each artist do it. Like an inside view, the making." I said.

She nodded and smiled. "I like the idea. It's like a studio documentary. Nice."

Xtasy

"Glad you agree. I was going to head to the studio where Belofant's setting up, you wanna accommodate me?" I held out my arm, she smiled and locked hers in mine. I thought nothing of it until I looked at her smile. She was beaming.

"Belo', glad you're back and ready. The world missed you." I said as I shook his hand.

"No doubt, I missed it all too. I just had a lot going on. Wifey was missing me, -"

I held up my hand stopping him. "Trust me, I understand. Rappers and singers have lives too. I feel you."

Belo' nodded. "I'm all set if y'all are. I got this song I wrote, called, 'A misconception of love: I think it's a hit.

"Well, let's hear it," I said as Belofante started for the booth. "Belo', wait." I stopped him. "We came up with the idea to record a recording session. Each artist will do one. So, show the world what they've been missing."

Belofante smiled before walking into the booth. I handed my phone to Trineka. "Go live, turn it off for nothing." She nodded.

I sat at the sound board beside the lead engineer. Belo' took his shirt off and tossed it to the floor. I knew he was about to kill it, marriage changes a man for the better. Love brings out the best in people

The beat started. It started off as a simple piano note; like Alicia Keys was playing it herself. Then the beat of a drum came, sounding like Anderson Pak. Then came Belofante's soft, hypnotizing smooth voice.

"A misconception of love is that it always brings pain/People swe-ar on their soul to-oo never love again./they say it's better to love and lost ... then to never love at all./but som-ee rather stay alone, then risk a fal-ll./a misconception of loveee ... is that it always end well/picket fence and a dog ... just like in fairy tales/but the truth of it all/you got to fight hard to keep her/go through heartache and pain to make her mean something deeper ... mis-con-ception of-fff lov-eee ..."

Trineka touched me, then placed the phone in my face. My Instagram was going bananas. The comments came and went in a blur only to be replaced by another then another. I don't think anyone loves their job more than me. I really loved my hob. I love music. Music is stronger than medicine. The true pain reliever. The soul healer.

Trineka kissed me on the cheek. "You're a genius!" She said excitedly. I was glad that the lights were dimmed, or she would've seen me blush.

***

-Trineka-

Belofante's studio recording was the talk of the net. The video was shared 1.4 million times. Belofante was right, the song was a hit. I was so excited for Belo'; I couldn't control my emotions. I kissed Cedrick's cheek congratulating him on the bright idea he came up with to record the session.

I think the kiss caught him off guard, but I knew he liked it. I saw it all over his face. Afterwards, he kinda blushed, I pretended not to see it. Belofante continued to sing until he had finished two other tracks, which outdid everything he ever wrote.

After the session, Cedrick escorted me back to my office so that I could upload the video on the company blog. I don't know what it was, but I seemed happier in his presence. Like nothing else seemed to exist.

"That was amazing, huh," I said as I sat in my computer chair.

"Yeah, I didn't see that coming," Ced said as he sat across from me. The way he looked at me, I couldn't tell if he was referring to the studio session or the kiss on the cheek.

"Yes, Belofante sounded amazing. His fans were going crazy over the new song. It won't be long before they're asking for an album."

"It'll have to be some heat because the song he just recorded set the bar." I nodded.

I started at Cedrick, wanting to approach the elephant in room, yet I didn't want to ruin the moment. But if I didn't it would always be on the forefront of his mind.

"Cedrick-" The same time I was calling his name, he had called mine. I couldn't stop the smile that appeared on my face.

"You go first," I said.

"No, ladies first." he insisted.

"No you, I would rather hear your idea first, I get a lot of good feedback from you."

"Okay. But it was more of a question though. But I'll go first. I noticed something about Belofante. His sound, his vibe, it was like he was singing from down deep, from his soul. He was singing for a greater purpose, something that's greater than life. Belofante was singing for love, his love, his family. Hearing him sing made me realize how special marriage is; how God blesses those who do. I was taking my time on Amy and me getting married. Hell, I haven't even bought the wedding ring yet. Now my question, is would you be my guest and help me in finding Amy the perfect wedding ring."

My smile faded, but I replaced it with a fake one just as fast. I hated life, not just mine, but everyone's. I just couldn't understand it, and I don't think I ever would. Here Cedrick was a very smart handsome man who's faithful, he's the perfect gentleman, and I could only imagine what he's like in bed. He does everything right, from the way he dresses, to opening up the door for me, to making my kitty wet without even trying. He's a way better man than Jason. And I could tell when he loves, he loves for real. Amy was lucky as hell. Better yet, she was extremely blessed. And I prayed every night, yet I feel like I've been cursed.

Cedrick asked me to accommodate him to help him find Amy a wedding ring. Of course, I would, but I would have my own agenda. "I'm happy for you Cedrick. Of course I'll go with you." I faked another smile as I updated the studio recording.

I was once told that a human's heart is where God and Satan prepare for war. I guess it was time for me to start feeding the

Moan in my Mouth

devil; because I didn't have any more Manna left in me to feed God.

$$$

Xtasy

Chapter 16
-Amy-

I hadn't seen Cupid since the last time he'd spent the night at our house. I'm lying, he was a constant guest in my dreams. It was more like a wet nightmare because I knew I shouldn't be dreaming about him, let alone lusting after his black snake man.

Cupid was Cedrick's best friend and his best man for the wedding. That was why I couldn't understand why Cupid did what he did. I started to expose him and tell Cedrick what he did because what he did was foul. But if what he did was foul, then I deserved a technical foul. I was just as guilty as him if not more. If we were sent to trial, Cupid would've got off on all charges for reasonable doubt, maybe he was asleep. But me, oh God, I just gave in to all sin. If I was a Catholic, I would be confessing to a priest for two days.

I had to go to work today. As much as I wanted to avoid Cupid, I couldn't. To not come to work, would make me look guilty. And I'm innocent until proven guilty. I had a trick up my stocking for Cupids as though. He wanted to play mind games, then I was down. One thing men failed to realize; we played better mind games. We invented it.

"Good, God!" Chad, the doorman blurted out. "I-I'm sorry, good morning Amy."

I smiled mischievously, if Chad reacted in that way, I couldn't wait to see Cupids' reaction. "Good morning to you too, Chad." I walked through the door he held open for me. I didn't bother to look back, I knew Chad was watching my every step.

Heads turned as I walked through the building to get to Cupid's office. I could feel the stares, the heat coming from their eyes as they roamed all over my body. As I made it to my desk, I took my coat off and laid it over the back of my chair. Cupid's office blinds were down, which meant he didn't want to be bothered.

I knocked on the door. He didn't answer. I pulled out the spare key that he had given me for emergencies. I placed it in the lock. This was definitely an emergency. I walked into the office.

Xtasy

Cupid had his cell phone to his ear deep in a conversation. The back of his chair was facing me. I cleared my throat to announce my presence. Cupid spun his chair around, his phone fell from his hand. His mouth opened; a soft, unexpected moan escaped. I looked at the package that got me in this predicament. The unexpected surprise package that I was forced to open with my eyes. The meaty package that took up all the space between his legs. The package had arrived. There was no point in ringing the doorbell, I knew it was coming. I had ordered it, sexual delivery.

***

-Cupid-

"Hello," I answered the unknown number that called.

"Hey," the soft voice said. "Is this Cupid?" She asked.

"This is, may I ask who's calling?" I looked at the screen, the number started with a 903 area code. I didn't know anyone from East Texas, I didn't think.

"This is Brianna. We met the other night at the Laker, Mavericks game."

I smiled. How could I forget the white woman with the hustler for a kid? And let's not forget her perfect apple bottom. I'm not an ass man, I'm a woman man. I love all women. But I do love a woman with an ass.

"Brianna, nice to hear your voice. How'd your son, Tristan?"

"He's doing good, he's actually right beside me."

"Tell him hello," I said. I could hear her tell him exactly what I said, and I heard him greet me back.

"He says hey, and he wants his action back." Brianna laughed as she referred the message.

I couldn't help but laugh too." Tell him, I wouldn't have it any other way. But let him know the stakes will be higher next time."

"Like what?" She asked without referring the message.

"Who knows, a one-on-one date with someone he knows." I smiled only because I figured she was probably smiling too.

Moan in my Mouth

"Wow, that's really high stakes. I don't know if his grandma will be available, but I'll ask her."
"I laughed at her sense of humor. "Good one, I like that."
"As you should." I agreed
"You have my number now. You may use it if you'd like."
"I would. In fact, I was actually going to go to Incredible Pizza later if you and Tristian wanna be my guest?"
"Really, you were going to Incredible Pizza, alone."
"Not really, but I figured a woman of your caliber wouldn't let me go alone."
"Who said I agreed to go?" She played along.
"I tell you what, put your phone on speaker."
"Okay. You're on speaker, now what?"
"Tristian!" I yelled
"Yes," he answered.
"If you go to Incredible Pizza with me, there will be unlimited tokens at your disposal. What do you say?"
"Oh ma, can I go?" Tristan yelled. I laughed. I knew I had won.
"That's not fair, Cupid." She said.
"Ma, he said unlimited," Tristan said.
"Okay. What time and where?" She gave in. I knew Tristian probably gave her his most puppy dog face. One she couldn't refuse.
"I'll text you the details -" I was saying as I heard something from behind me.

I spun my chair to see who had walked in unannounced. I was sure I had locked the door, and my blinds were down, everyone knew what my blinds down meant. I didn't want to be bothered. The only way someone was able to come in, was if they had a key. The only people who had a key were myself, and Amy.

As soon as I saw who it was, my mouth fell open, my cell phone slipped from my hand, and my eyes bucked. Amy stood before me, her skirt was short, stopping above her knee, tight as I've ever seen. Her blouse was even tighter. Two buttons were unbuttoned. Her laced bra showing, and her twins sitting up perfectly. She looked great. Like a slutty secretary. My slutty secretary.

My eyes roamed all over her body, I couldn't control OG as he tried to be nosey and see what all the excitement was about. Amy didn't say anything to me, her eyes traveled to OG, she looked, then looked away as she walked off towards my office restroom. I picked my phone up from the floor.

"I'll text you the details, and I'll see you later." I didn't wait for Brianna to respond as I hung up and sat my phone on the desk.

I fixed OG so he wouldn't be showing as much. The feeling was uncomfortable, but it would save me from a lawsuit. I walked to the bathroom standing on the outside wanting to go in, but knowing better.

Amy was cleaning up the restroom, her ass was in the air as I walked up; she was wiping the toilet down with Lysol wipes. Her ass was well-rounded. I couldn't see a panty line, which made me jealous. G-strings were so lucky, always having the chance to be all up in a woman's glory.

Amy cleaned the toilet, her ass swayed as she did. I silently prayed that it never got cleaned. Amy finished and turned around. "Good morning." She smiled.

I nodded. My words had abandoned me when I needed them the most. Traitors! "I saw how filthy the toilet was the last time I'd used it, so I put it on my to-do list." She said,

I closed my eyes and prayed that she put me on her to-do list. Please lord!

I stood in the doorway as she began to wipe down the sink and counter. As her arms moved, her titties moved side to side. I stared my mouth watered. I looked, no, stared at the purple vein that looked exotic on them, the lifeline to them, the blood flow.

Amy dropped a cleaning wipe. She turned her back to me, bent over and grabbed it. I could see the back of her thigh, the thickness, the smoothness, the only thing supporting her fat juicy ass. I was convinced she got her peaches from Georgia; I doubted her mother had anything to do with all that ass.

Moan in my Mouth

I had to close my eyes, the sight was just too much. When I opened them, Amy was walking out of the restroom. My mind told me to move, but my legs felt like silly putty. Amy walked past me, her soft skin brushed against OG; her sweet perfume invaded my third sense. The smell was intoxicating.

When my legs finally decided to obey me, Amy was behind my desk wiping everything down. She leaned over my laptop, her twins looked as if they were contemplating suicide, threatening to jump overboard. I prayed for their safe landing.

Please, Lord!

Amy grabbed my suit jacket that rested on the back of my chair and hung it on the coat rack. I took that as my cue to have a seat. It was either sit or let her see OG break out of prison.

As I sat down, Amy began to fix the paperwork on my desk, neither of us saying anything. Her being focused on the task at hand, and me trying my hardest to stay focused. A piece of paper fell on my side on the floor, I scooted my chair back to grab it; Amy came around the desk beating me to it.

Amy got on her knees in front of me. My legs were apart, I looked down at her, she grabbed the paper then looked up at me. "I'm so clumsy." She said.

All I could do was nod, my words were cowards. I could feel something sticky, slowly slide down OG, bastard threw up like a kid does when he can't hold his liquor. Amy stood up and faced the desk as she reorganized the fallen paperwork. Her ass was within something reach. All I had to do was lean forward and take a sniff.

Against my better judgment, I did exactly that. I sniffed hard, yet quietly so she wouldn't catch me. My good awesome Lord, she smelled amazing. I guess I wasn't an ass man after all. Amy finished her task and walked to the opposite side of the desk.

"All finished." She said then looked at how OG had stretched my fitted pants. "If you need anything, just call, I'll be outside."

I nodded. It was all I could do.

$$$

Xtasy

Chapter 17
-Cedrick-

Work went great. Trineka agreed to go with me to find Amy's wedding ring. Instead of going today, we scheduled to go Friday during our lunch break. When I asked her, she hesitated but she agreed. I couldn't thank her enough, she was a life saver.

I beat Amy home again. Instead of cooking. I ordered Chinese food. I logged onto my Instagram to see everyone's comments from Belofantes recording session. My phone had been vibrating all day with notifications. I was so busy I wasn't able to check the comments.

I smiled as I strolled through the comments. Everyone was congratulating Belofante and showing their support for his comeback. I kept scrolling through the comments with a smile on my face. That was until I came across a comment.

:Nice song Belofante. Who's the hottie kissing you Cedrick? Hook a brother up!

I scrolled down to see similar comments asking about the woman, and the kiss. I read the comments confused as to what they were talking about. I went back up to the video and pressed play. I watched Belofante's performance like I wasn't there to see it live. I was glad to be a part of his movement.

As I watched the video, the camera moved from Belo' I could hear Trineka call me a genius. The camera flipped. For the world to see, Trineka's lips touched my cheek. And sadly, the camera caught me blushing. I parsed the video and scrolled down the new comments. People were saying how good we looked together.

I slapped my forehead with the palm of my hand. I knew the bad publicity this would bring when people found out who she really was, especially being engaged to Jason. I could only hope Amy hadn't seen the video already so that I'll be able to explain myself.

The front door opened. Amy tossed her keys on the table. I ran to meet her. "How was work?" I asked. She gave me a sour look that only answer my suspicion.

Xtasy

"So, you're disrespecting me for the whole world to see?"

I tried to kiss her cheek but she moved out of reach.

"Don't try to kiss me. Explain yourself. Do you know how embarrassing that is. My fiance, getting a kiss on Instagram live. You're friends with my whole family for God's sake!"

Amy stormed off to our bedroom. "I can explain," I said as I followed her.

"I bet! You know every man says that once they've been caught red-handed."

"Come on Amy. What have I been caught doing? It was only a kiss on the cheek. A congrats kiss. Nothing serious about it, I swear."

'So a woman kisses you on camera, live, it's nothing serious. Well, I'll tell you what. You're sleeping in your man cave tonight, that's how serious it is to me!"

I tried to grab her to tell her I was sorry, but she yanked away from me. "Get out! I just need a night alone. Please!"

I nodded. It was the least I could do. I didn't want to make the situation worse than it was. I walked out of the bedroom and headed down to my man cave. We hadn't even said "I do" yet, and I was already sleeping on the couch.

***

-Cupid-

"Okay Tristian, stay where I can see you, and remember, you have school tomorrow, so we're not staying all night." Brianna lectured him.

Tristan nodded with a cup full of tokens in his hand.

"Okay ma! Can I go now?" Tristan asked.

Brianna smiled and nodded. "Go ahead." She watched him walk away as if he was going off to college.

I laughed, breaking her trance. "What's so funny?" She asked.

Moan in my Mouth

"You. The way you're watching him like he's never coming back."

"Did I, really?" She asked.

I nodded as I took a sip from my soda. "It's fine, it shows how much you care."

"I really do. He's my one and only. My first and last breath. I'm just enjoying it all while he's still young. Everything changes when they grow older."

"How you figure?"

"Life. It scares me. This world is cruel. At his age, life seems innocent. Even that's changing. Nowadays, people are shooting up schools left and right without care. Every day while he's at school and my phone rings, my heart jumps and I fear for him when he gets older. The way police are killing innocent black men, I fear for my son. They don't see a mixed kid, he'll be black."

I nodded. I didn't look at life that way, probably because I didn't have any kids. "I couldn't agree with you more. Tristan will be a great kid, I can already see it. He's smart, polite, and he has a great teacher." She smiled. "Thank you. I wish his father would see what you see."

"I didn't want to be the one to bring the subject up, but since you did, why isn't he around?"

"Because he's a jerk." She said.

I smiled. "I guess that sums it all up."

"I'm sorry," she sighed. "It's because he claims he wasn't ready. When I got pregnant, he wanted me to have an abortion, but I refused.

"I'm glad you did. Tristian's a great kid." I said as he was running up to me with a huge smile on his face.

"Cupid, look. There's a game with your name on it." He smiled and pulled me towards the game.

Brianna walked with us as she smiled the whole way.

"See!" Tristan pointed to the Cupid shooting game.

Brianna smiled. "Have you played it yet?" I asked him. He shook his head. "Do you know why it's called, Cupid's Arrows?"

He shook his head again. "Cupid was the God of love. Do you know what love means?"

"I love my mom." He said innocently.

"Yes, but this love is for another person other than your mom. Do you have a girl in your class that you think is pretty?"

Tristan looked at his mother. "Don't mind your mother, it's only us men talking right now." Tristan smiled at my comment.

"There's Brandy, she sits beside me in class."

"How do you think she looks?" I asked.

"Like my mom," he said.

"So she's beautiful," I said. Tristan nodded. "Does Brandy make you feel weird around her, like shy or scared?"

"How'd you know?" He asked surprised.

"I am Cupid," the God of love." Brianna smiled and shook her head. "Cupid, the God of love would find two random people, and shoot them with love darts, forcing them to love each other. I've shot you with a love dart, I've just been taking my time shooting Brandy."

Tristian got excited. "So, you're going to shoot her, so that she'll love me like I love her?"

"Well, it depends."

"Aw'l come on Cupid," he whined.

"How're your grades in school?" I asked.

"I got all A's, and one C on my report card."

"I tell you what. If you can bring that C, up to a B, I'll shoot Brandy with a dart too."

"Ma, did you hear that, did you hear that! Brandy's going to love me. Thank ya, Cupid!" Tristan hugged me.

I looked at Brianna, she stared at me, I had shot her with an arrow without even trying.

$$$

Chapter 18
-Amy-

"Amy, you're here early," Cupid said as he walked into his office. He hung his jacket on the coat rack and walked around his desk.

"I figured I'll come in early, get a head start. You know, catch up on some things." Cupid sat down behind his desk and powered up his laptop.

"Is something bothering you?" He asked.

I sighed and said. "I and Ced got into an argument last night."

"What about?"

"A video he had on Instagram live." Cupid laughed. "What was on the video?"

"A woman kissing him on the cheek," I said. Cupid laughed again.

"You got upset about him getting a kiss on the cheek," he said as he stood up.

"It wasn't just about the kiss," I said defensively. Cupid walked behind me.

"What else was it then?" Cupid asked as his hands went to my shoulders. They were tense, but under his touch, they loosened up.

"The woman, she was beautiful," I said as he began to work his magic with his hands.

"So you were jealous of her?"

I nodded, then quickly shook my head. "She was pretty, I meant."

Cupid laughed. "Is that right? So, if you're beautiful, and she's only pretty, then why were you jealous?"

I shrugged. "I don't know."

"How could you be mad at Ced for getting a kiss on the cheek when we've been doing the most."

"What are you talking about?" I asked. Cupid stopped his magical hands and turned me to him.

Xtasy

"You know what I'm talking about," he said, walking closer to me. I backed backwards, stopping as the desk sandwiched me between Cupid and his growing hard-on.

Cupid eased closer to me and kissed my cheek. "Now, y'all are even. Let's up the ante," he said as he kissed me softly on the lips. It caught me off guard, but when he unzipped his pants and shoved my hand inside, that caught me by surprise.

As our kiss broke off, I caught myself. My hand was massaging his massive dick through his zipper. "Cupid, this is so wrong," I moaned as he kissed me again.

"How does it feel?" He asked.

"It fee-feels good and strong." Cupid eased my skirt up my legs, I could've sworn I had worn some panties, yet I stood before him naked.

"You know, everything happens for a reason. Cedrick gave you to me." Cupid said as he inched his hand towards my kitty. I watched his hand as it neared my slit.

"How did he give you to me?" I asked as his finger split my sex lips. I shook my head. "I mean, how-w did he give me to , oh shit. You!"

Cedrick strummed my clit like BBKing does Lucille. I knew what he was doing was dead wrong, but the way it felt, God the way it felt.

"He practically handed you to me on a silver platter. I own a porn industry-" I stopped him mid-sentence.

"The number one porn industry," I said, making him smile.

"I stand corrected. I own the number one professional film company. Yet your husband -"

"Fiance." I stopped him again.

"Yes, fiance. Your fiance let you come and be my secretary. He knew what could happen, what would happen."

As he talked, he worked my clit with expertise. I see why he went into the porn industry, he knew every way to curve his finger, every word to say, and he spoke softly, convincing. My eyes closed, then opened again.

Moan in my Mouth

Cupid's dick was in my hand, so big, and strong; heavy. I held it, but it had control over me, like taking an untrained dog for a walk. I stroked him, my legs parted on their own. Cupid's dick inched closer to my center, my mind was telling me no, but the wetness between my legs told me I'd be a damn fool not to.

"Cupid," I panted as he leaned forward to kiss me. I looked between my legs, it looked as if his dick was kissing my kitty.

"You won't regret it, I promise," Cupid said as his dick nuzzled its way between my sex lips.

I gasped and closed my eyes, we were really doing it. Fucking. My fiance's best friend. His best man. The one he grew up with.

I opened my eyes at the sudden pressure that my kitty was feeling. Cupid's dick had expanded, stretched, and it looked to be getting bigger. I thought I was going crazy because his dick was getting bigger.

"Cupid, what-what's going on, with." my words tripped over the next clumsy as I watched his dick grow in width and length.

Cupid's eyes closed, then opened, his eyes were like Michael Jackson's in the video, Thriller. I tried to move away from his python as it pushed inside me. The feeling was a mixture of pain and utter pleasure. My walls stretched, swallowed his dick like the last bite of snicker. My hands went to his chest, the pain, the pleasure, the mixture.

"Cu-Cupid! We're so wrong!" Even though I said, it I didn't want him to stop.

Cupid kept pounding inside of me, rotating his hips like a hoola hoop. The alarm went off on his phone, he stopped his hoola hoop stroke and picked up his phone.

"Why'd you stop?" I asked.

"Because it's time for you to wake up," He said.

I looked at him confused, he showed me the screen of his phone. The screen read! Time for work.

I jumped out of my sleep and snatched my phone up. The alarm I had set for work was going off. I turned it off and looked around. I was in bed alone, and I was glad. God only knows what I was saying in my sleep. I threw the covers off of me, there was a

115

puddle under my ass, sticky, and wet. My panties were soaked; sticky as well.

I sat up in bed, my legs were like jello, like I had actually had sex for real. The dream felt real, exotic, and wrong. I was glad it was just a dream. I thought Cupid was a nice guy, but I was engaged, and I loved my fiance Cedrick. I honestly did.

Why was I having dreams about his best friend? That's a question I don't want to answer. That's why I'm glad Ced slept in his mancave, or I would have some explaining to do. There's nothing more embarrassing than having to answer questions you don't know the answers to.

I quickly discarded my cum soaked panties and stepped into a fresh pair. I left the bedroom and walked to Ced's man cave. I just wanted to see his face, to kiss him, and tell him I forgive him for how I reacted.

I crept downstairs, his projector was still on from him up late last night. I looked at the screen, the video had been playing, but it was paused. I muted the TV and pressed play. Cedrick appeared on the screen, he was blushing, like a high school girl. I don't have to remind you what made him blush. But I rewinded it a couple of seconds for my own benefit. I watched the kiss on the cheek, Ced blushing then smiling.

I looked at Cedrick as he slept in his favorite chair. The chair made for men, the lazy boy. The chair where men get lost in their sports, or in Ced's case, lost in lust. Cedrick slept in his chair, a big smile was on his face. I followed his hands with my eyes. His hand was covering his hard-on. I guess I wasn't the only one who had a good dream.

$$$

Chapter 19
-Cedrick-

I woke up in my man cave, the place I asked for so I and some of my close friends could have fellas night, yet it turned into a bedroom overnight, my bedroom. Amy got upset at me for the video Trineka had posted all over the internet. Not that it was her fault; I was the one who told her to record the studio session, so she was only doing what she was told. The video wasn't really the issue, it was the kiss that happened during the recording. I didn't see what all the fuss was about it; it was only a kiss on the cheek.

Amy made a big deal about it; like I deliberately tried to embarrass her. She was so upset, she made me sleep in my man cave. It got under my skin that she didn't let me explain myself, not like I had much to explain being that the video was there to see what Amy was so upset about. It looked like a simple kiss, one on the cheek at that. It wasn't like we had swapped spit. The only thing that got me was how I blushed when she did it; that part was embarrassing. Now the whole world would know me as a blusher.

When I woke up, I noticed the video was still on the projector playing on repeat. I must've fallen asleep watching it. I stood up and stretched my back popped. My lazy boy had me sleeping like a baby. I picked up my phone and looked at the time, I was late for work. I guess I slept too good. I stormed up the stairs in a hurry; I hated being late. I walked through the kitchen to get to the bedroom, I smelt eggs in the air, but there were none in sight. I walked into the bedroom, Amy was nowhere in sight either. Our bed was completely made up, nothing out of place. I knew she had already left, we had to be at work at the same time. What I couldn't understand was how she could let me oversleep. I understand she was upset, but to let me oversleep was doing the most.

My phone vibrated with a text message from Trineka.
: if you caught a flat, don't be afraid to ask for help. ;)
I shot her a quick text back saying how I stopped for doughnuts for the staff, and I'll be right in. After sending the text, I

117

shook my head as I rushed to get dressed. Now I would have to buy doughnuts for the whole staff. Thanks Amy!

***

-Trineka-

    Cedrick was late, which was a first. It was a good thing Jason was out of town on business. Crazy thing, Jason took Brandi with him. He claimed she was needed being that she was his secretary and all. But what did she know about Bloody Lyrics that I didn't know? I wasn't a fool, my mama raised me.
    After texting Cedrick, my mind went back to the kiss. Even though it was on the cheek, it meant something to me. I was glad I got it all on recording, I watched it so many times I could picture it every time I closed my eyes. And the comments, people were calling us a cute couple. I didn't respond to clear up the rumors, I was enjoying it. I doubt if Jason has seen the video, or he would've called demanding us to take it down. Too bad he's gone on 'business'.
    I walked to the front entrance, I was right on time as Cedrick walked through the door with five dozen Krispy Kreme doughnuts, which were my favorite.
    "Good morning, slowpoke." I teased him as he carried the doughnuts to the conference room. I walked behind him as he tried to balance the boxes in one hand while holding his Gucci briefcase in the other hand.
    As he went to sit the boxes on the table, his briefcase fell from his hand and hit the floor, opening up. "Damn!" he spat.
    I kneeled to catch his important papers before they began to scatter. Cedrick kneeled with me, picking the whole briefcase up. I looked at the papers I held in my hand. "Cedrick, are these yours? Like, did you write them?" I continued to read his amazing work.
    Cedrick sat the briefcase on the table and said. "Yes, I wrote it, but it's nothing."

Moan in my Mouth

I looked at him. "This is something, this is amazing wh-why didn't you tell me you wrote like this?"

"Because, it's just a poem, nothing serious." He grabbed the papers and tossed them into his suitcase.

"Are you ashamed of what you wrote, I mean, you shouldn't be. People would pay for work like that."

Cedrick only nodded as he reorganized his papers in his briefcase, I could feel something was off about his vibe, he wouldn't even look at me.

"Cedrick is everything okay?" I asked as he pretended to not hear me. "Cedrick," I said his name again.

"No!" Cedrick shouted as he shoved his briefcase halfway across the table. His sudden outburst caught me by surprise, causing me to flinch.

"I-I'm sorry for," I said as he cut me off, anger in his eyes.

"Did you know you had recorded yourself kissing me on the cheek?" he asked.

I shook my head. "No, if I would've known, I wouldn't have done it."

Cedrick looked at me, a million and one thoughts running through his mind, and not one I could read. "Amy saw the video, she was heated, so mad that she made me sleep on the couch, she wouldn't even let me explain."

"What was there to explain?" The kiss was nothing, I mean it was on the cheek for God's sake."

"That's what I was trying to explain to her, but she wouldn't let me. It was innocent, just a congrats kiss."

I nodded only because he was looking at me. His part was innocent, but me, I was guilty as charged, no need to deliberate. "Do you think she has trust issues?"

"No, Amy. I-no." He stuttered.

"You don't sound so sure yourself."

Cedrick looked at me and said, "She trusts me, we're getting married, remember."

I smiled. "No need to remind me, you should remind her."

"What did Jason have to say about it?"

"He didn't say anything about the kiss?"

"No," I smiled. "I and Jason will be exchanging vows soon. In order to say 'I do,' you have to have trust. Jason could leave his phone around the house, and I would never go through it, and vice versa."

Cedrick nodded, his mind drifted off. I knew the seed was planted, with water, it would grow. But a bad seed only produces bad fruit. Thank God for the farmer!

$$$

Chapter 20
-Cupid-

I came prepared today, after the last encounter with Amy, I had to be on point. The last time she left me hot and bothered, sticky, and beyond horny as hell. So today, I decided to wear two pairs of boxer briefs. I know doing so, I went against my beliefs of keeping OG cool, but either way, Amy made him hot.

Amy's show had been on my mind all night. I had got a call last night from Brianna. Tristan had wanted to bet on the New Orleans Pelicans game, against the Mavericks. The wager would be another game night at Incredible Pizza, if he won. He talked me into it only by giving me ten points. Luckily the Mavs won by eight, helping me to score a cooked dinner at their house. We made arrangements for tonight and honestly, I was looking forward to it. Tristan was an awesome kid, and Brianna, a helluva catch.

"Cupid, everything is set up in studio room one, whenever you're ready," Amy said, peeping her head in the room.

I made it a point to keep my distance from Amy, at all costs. She came to work with yet another short, short skirt. Her button-down was skin tight, the A/C made her nipples stand to attention like an army brat. Every time she would come into my office to grab something, I would look the other way, or close my eyes. Closing my eyes never worked, it would only make it worse as images of her glorious body would appear.

I nodded at Amy, "Give me a sec' I'll meet you there."

Amy nodded before closing the door back. I went to the restroom, I had to do the ritual'. "Before every recording, I would be tired, so when the actors got to recording, I would be the only one in the room without a hard-on. People thought I had total control over OG, that I could make him wake up and go to sleep at will. Waking up, yes. But going to sleep, he was like a kid. I would have to tire him out first, get him exhausted, then he'll pass out wherever he lay.

Xtasy

I closed the restroom door and sat on the toilet, pants covering my knees. I unlocked my iPhone, I went to Google and searched for 'KKvsh. There was just something about the caramel beauty. The way she had the full, God-given package. Ass, titties, and a mondo burger between her legs. When she started off on Only Fans, I was sure I was her biggest fan.Secretively, I spent thousands to see her dance, call me a trick, but I was rewarded with a hella-fide treat.

I scrolled to my favorite video of her, the one where she's lying in front of the camera, legs wide open, like Satan's demons were holding her legs open for her. There was nothing sexier than a woman pleasing herself, getting herself off, imagining God knows what so she could accomplish her mind-blowing, screaming orgasm.

I turned the audio down, but only enough so no one else could hear. I pressed play, spread my legs and assumed the position. I gripped OG like a gun, held him steady hands ready to pull the trigger. as I watched KKvsh get herself wet, OG looked amazed, like he was seeing the video for the first time.

As KKvsh got her sex lips slippery with her own juices, I licked my lips, preparing for a kiss she would never receive from me. I worked the skin back and forth on OG, slowly, yet intensely. Masturbating was the training ground for how a man performs in bed. If you're a quick stroker, you'll be a quick pumper.

As KKvsh moaned to the rhythm of her manicured hands, so did I. She was a piece of art that I was captivated by. A painting, a masterpiece. In order to appreciate real art, you have to really look at it, the picture so you know what the artist was feeling, was thinking. I felt her vibes, the built-up pressure, wanting to be released, set free, no bond stipulations.

I closed my eyes, I could feel my balls tighten, the pressure squeezing them to be released, so I squeezed the head of OG, pushing the pressure back down. I wanted to nut at the same time as she did, the art of seduction.

I closed my eyes, slowly pumping OG, raising my hand up and down him, stopping at the top with a closed fist, like I was at a

Moan in my Mouth

black live matter movement. My eyes opened as the restroom door opened. I was caught red-handed, or in my case, dick-handed. Off instinct, I tried to pull my pants up, which was the whole point of having them on my knees, quick access.

Karen walked into the restroom and closed the door behind herself, doing what I should've done in the beginning, locking it. She stood before me, wanting and beautiful. She was like my sex angel, always there when I needed her. She stood before me with a yellow sundress on my favorite attire for a woman to wear. Somehow, I think she knew it.

Sundresses just did something to my soul. The way they were made to sit perfectly on top of a woman's ass, yet stop low enough to leave you wanting more. The way the helms bounced when they walked. And let's not forget the easy access.

"Karen, h-how did you get in here?" I asked, pants still hiding OG.

"I walked through the door," she smiled, then licked her lips.

"But, why are you here?"

"I came to pick up my last check." She looked deep between my legs, trying to see OG, to witness his most glorious moments.

"You know your checks go direct deposit, so stop playing." I looked at her, the way her sundress squeezed her twins together. The way I could see she didn't have any panties on.

"Do you want me to go?" She asked, walking closer to me like I was the door.

She stood over me, her hand went down to OG, I didn't stop her, didn't object or put up a fight. She found OG, in his hiding spot, hoping to be hidden again, this time in a warmer place, one that's wet, and tight.

Karen stroked him, taking her time, like we weren't in a workplace. "I missed you so damn much," she said. I wasn't sure if she was talking to me, or OG.

I pulled my pants down to my ankles, she stepped between my legs, I sniffed slowly, inhaling her perfume. I had a habit of doing that, I guess it was just the dog in me, the way the sweet scent of a woman could set me off like an alarm.

Xtasy

Karen stroked OG, I lightly bit her mound through the fabric of her dress. I raised it from the back, the feel of her bare smooth bottom, pantyless, just like I figured. I stood, her hand still holding OG, afraid to let him go. I grabbed her by the waist, carried her to the door, and held her up in the air. She didn't need me to explain what to do next, some lessons were taught through experience.

Karen grabbed OG, reaching behind herself she worked the head of him inside her hole. OG was good at playing hide and seek. Karen's sundress hid her luscious ass, we stayed still for a moment, basking in the way she felt, the way OG felt inside her. I placed her back against the restroom door, she let out a grunt, but it was soon replaced with soft passionate moans as I pumped in and out of her.

Karen had some amazing pussy, probably the best I've ever had. But good pussy was only good until you could find better pussy. This was why I had to make this our last time, for both of our sakes.

"Cupid, my God, you feel me up, so-ooo, good. I-I love it." She moaned as she kissed all over my face. Tongue slid in my mouth, our spit swapped, like a fair exchange. I tongued her, she tongued me. At the same time, I raised the back of her dress, gripped her ass, held on to it like a set of bicycle handles, enjoying the ride.

My hand moved between the crease of her cheeks, together, yet separate. I worked my thumb to a place the world never saw, the hole that was the tightest. My thumb explored, moved around the crevice, searching for the opening, hoping to find gold, the hidden treasure.

Karen's lip-locking was halted as she felt my thumb break through her backdoor like a thief in the night. Her eyes shot open wide, like she was seeing her life flash before her eyes.

"Fuck-kk, my asshole, God my asshole. Yess!" She screamed. I kissed her to smother her moans. I leaned back, holding her, yet using the door for support.

Moan in my Mouth

I watched as OG dove in and out of her wetness; like he was preparing for the Olympics. The nine-inch dash. Her hole opened, gripped, and pulled at OG all at the same time. I could understand why sex without being married was a sin, sex was a beautiful thing, hoty, sanctified, and pure. Such a feeling of an orgasm would make the angels sing.

"You're the fuckin' best, God you're, fuck, a God!" Karen yelled as I stuck my thumb deeper in her backdoor.

I felt OG getting bigger, the veins pumping blood faster than ever, his twin brother swelling, preparing to release. I slowed my pumps, careful not to let go inside of her, my legs twitched as the feeling became too sensitive.

"Here it cums, ohhh, Cupid!" Karen yelled as loud as she could. As soon as I felt her walls tighten around OG, I started to pick her up, so I could cum over her sexy ass cheeks.

As I held her up, her body shook like she was experiencing the holy ghost! I aimed to sit her down, but a sound against the door made me drop her, her legs weren't strong enough to support her, and the orgasm, so she fell to the floor. As she squirmed on the restroom floor, I listened for the sound again. The sound that messed up my rhythm.

I started to unlock the door, to open it and see what ruined my performance. With Karen shaking on the floor, I couldn't. I looked at Karen and shook my head. She always got like that, like a friend who claims she can handle her liquor, yet throws up every time leaving me to hold her hair.

I stood over Karen, her eyes were closed. I lightly slapped her cheeks to bring her back. Her eyes opened. The first thing she saw was OG, dangling over her face. She looked, then passed out.

Fucking lightweight!

***

-Amy-

Xtasy

As I was closing Cupid's office door, Karen walked up behind me wearing this very cute sundress. I could look at her and tell she wasn't wearing any panties. "Karen, hey!" I played it off like I was happy to see her.

Karen looked me up and down; from the way she looked, I could tell she didn't approve of my outfit. I didn't care for one, because I didn't approve of her ugly ass heels with such a pretty dress.

"Hey Amy. Is Cupid around?" Karen asked, already looking past me towards Cupids' office.

"Yes, he actually just went to the restroom, we're getting ready to record in studio one."

"Oh that's great, maybe he'll let me sit in and watch."

I stepped to the side, I could tell by the look in her eyes that nothing was going to stop her from going into Cupid's office. She wore her sundress for a reason. I gave her a half-smile to clear the awkwardness.

"I'ma go check on him, let him know I'm here," Karen said.

I nodded and walked off, looking back over my shoulder as Karen walked into his office. I took off in the direction of the studio, but I forgot the new script Cupid was working on. I quickly walked to his office, I thought for sure the door would be locked, but it wasn't.

I lightly knocked on the door, a small double knock no one answered, so I opened the door as I double knocked again. As I walked inside, I closed the door behind myself. Karen, nor Cupid were in sight. He didn't have my other exits, so they both had to be in the restroom.

I closed the blinds, everyone knew exactly what the blinds being closed meant. I then rushed to Cupid's desk to find the new script before either of them walked out of the restroom. As I was flipping through his stack of papers, I overheard soft moans coming from the restroom.

I blushed and continued my search. I found what I was looking for tucked inside a drawer. I fixed the papers back and went to the door to leave. As I grabbed the handle, a loud thump sounded

Moan in my Mouth

from the restroom, Karen moaned again and said something I couldn't make out.

Something told me to leave, to mind my own business. My curiosity got the best of me as Karen said, "Cupid, my god, you feel me up, so-ooo, good. I-I love it."

Something happened to me at that moment. I don't know what it was, but I felt it, like a switch was turned on inside of me, my inner freak. A tingle, like a shot of electricity shot to my clit, my legs shut automatically, my eyes closed. I held on to the doorknob, fighting the inner freak inside of me, putting up a fight, but not strong enough for my opponent.

I yanked away from the doorknob, mad at it for no apparent reason. My leg moved on its own, my mind too occupied with thoughts of Cupid and Karen. I walked slowly to the door, not believing I was actually doing what I was doing. I placed both palms on the door, paced my ear to it and listened. All that could be heard was skin slap skin, and my anxious, nervous heart.

My hand traveled under my shirt, slowly easing my wet thong to the side. My pussy was so wet, warm, and sensitive. I closed my eyes as I played with my clit. I imagined I was in the restroom with them, a camcorder in hand, directing them like my own porno, a porn-com.

I jumped, caught by surprise as Karen said, "Fuck-kk, my asshole, God, my asshole. Yess!"

My fingers worked faster, images of Cupid barging in Karen's backdoor flooded my mind. His log of a penis, better yet, his tongue, God, his finger. I wondered how it felt, did it cause pain or a jolt of pure ecstasy? Ced never inserted his dick inside my asshole, for his own manly reasons. Cedrick said it was gay. I didn't see how. I applauded Cupid on being an ass man.

"You're the fuckin' best, God you're, fuck, a God!" Karen moaned so loud I just knew someone else other than me heard.

I stuck my fingers in my mouth, tasting the wetness between my thighs. I went back to my clit, working my hands faster as I listened to Cupid fuck some sense into Karen. I felt it, the

127

pressure, the waves smacking up against the levees, demanding to be released.

"Here it cums, ohhh, Cupid!" Karen yelled, saying exactly what I was thinking.

Something inside of me exploded, the levees broke, the wetness that flooded my hand splashed. The feeling was unlike anything I've ever felt. I couldn't control the squirting liquid that seemed to come out of nowhere. My legs felt weak; my head dizzy. I tried to balance myself, but I couldn't. I leaned against the door, my head landed against it, causing a thump.

I cursed the freak inside of me for being so clumsy, so careless. I moved my thong to the side, fixed my skirt and rushed to the office door. I had to rush to grab the script, then I left, abandoned my post. I closed the door back moving quickly to the elevator. I pressed the elevator button, tapping my heel against the marble floor impatiently.

The elevator opened and I rushed inside happy it was isolated. I leaned my back against the wall, exhaled and smiled. As the doors closed, I felt cum sliding down my leg. I stuck my hand between my legs to catch it before it fell. I stuck my finger in my mouth, savored the saltiness, imagining it was a mixture of mine and Cupids.

I shook my head as I realized what I had just done. As the elevator opened, I shrugged my shoulders and walked off. It wasn't like I had had sex with Cupid yet.

$$$

Chapter 21
-Cedrick-

"Drill, you have to put everything into this track. Passion, thirst, you have to be hungry for this, crave it. Want it."

The rapper Drill nodded as he stood in the booth. Drill was a simple rapper in appearance, never one to flaunt how much money he had. He was content with flaunting one thing, his music. His style was a mixture of J Cole and Kendrick Lamar. He didn't rap about the things he didn't have or things he never saw. Drill's lyrics reflected life's problems, the earl, the authentic, the now, which was why he was signed to Bloody Lyrics.

"From the top Drill, ready?" I asked him.

Drill nodded, I reset the track from the top. Drill bobbed his head to the beat. He closed his eyes, getting a feel for a track that would either make or break his career.

"Life might be hard right now/so I'm praying for the streets and the war night now/I will never turn my back like my family/never lost my sanity, coherent all I hear is money/never be a casualty/just took a lost right now/behind bars chassin' dreams, I need God right now/For all the people that you lose, do you wonder why you're here/are you chassin' life or death for a spot that disappears./"

I bobbed my head as Drill spit the truth. I looked over my shoulder as Trineka walked into the room. A smile came to my face, force of habit. "Drill, take ten," I said into the sound system. Drill nodded as he took his headphones off.

"What's up?" I said as Trineka took a seat on the black leather couch.

"I just wanted to apologize for being careless, not paying attention to what I was recording, and for causing trouble between you and Amy."

I sat on the edge of my seat, pulled her hand in mine and said," You shouldn't be the one apologizing, it should be me. The way I treated you this morning was way out of line. You were only being supportive, something my own fiance has neglected to do, so let me apologize.

Trineka smiled and said. "You're an amazing man Cedrick, I know you didn't mean much by it. This job, mixed with being engaged, it's stressful, trust me I know," she smiled again. "You have to learn how to keep the two separate, balanced."

I nodded, she was right. Being the A&R director had caused a lot of stress, that, and Amy altogether. It was like when I needed her the most, she was nowhere to be found. Between me working, and her working later almost every night we rarely got a chance to talk like we did before she started working for Cupid. Even though it was the one that insisted. She worked for Cupid, now, I regretted it.

"What are you thinking about?" She asked, bringing me back to reality.

"Everything," I said.

"Like?" She said not letting me get off easily.

"I can't help but wonder if Amy trusts me or not. I know trust is everything in a marriage." Trineka shook her head and said," Trust isn't everything. Love is everything. Do you love her?" She asked.

I nodded, "Without a doubt."

"So what are you waiting on," she said excitedly.

"What do you mean?" She caught me off guard.

"Why wait until another season to marry her. All a woman wants is her knight in shining armor. Yea, she may want a huge wedding or maybe she wants you to take the initiative and take over, to say to hell with waiting, let's get married now."

A huge smile came to my face, Trineka was right. I don't know how I'd missed the signs. "You're right!" I said smiling. "I'm the man, the pants, the head of the house, king of the castle. I should've been taking the initiative to make her Mrs. Amy Montgomery." I stood up, proud, excited, and determined.

"So you're going to do it, you're going to speed the process up and get her to marry you sooner?"

I nodded, "Yes! But first, I have to buy a wedding ring."

Moan in my Mouth

Trineka stood up full of excitement for me. "I'm handed to help you pick the perfect ring for the perfect woman."

"Let's go now, I don't wanna waste another moment."

I said, then went to the soundboard. "Drill, take the rest of the day off, I got a wedding to plan!"

Drill looked at me confused, I grabbed Trineka's hand and pulled her behind me, she was all smiles.

***

-Cupid-

It took me close to an hour to finally get Karen off the restroom floor. When she finally came out, she had gained her strength back, her courage, ready for round two. I sent her home, I wasn't interested in another round, knowing I had already knocked her out before.

After cleaning her scent off of me, I finally headed off to studio one where everything was fully set up for a film I had put together called, 'Moan In My Mouth'. The plot was about a sexual friendship that got out of hand. A friendship that started off similar to Amy and me; being introduced to each other through mutual friends. The two main characters, Bryan and Sabrina work together on a project that neither is interested in working on. They both feel as if the task is a downgrade from what they're used to working on. The whole time Bryan and Sabrina's working on their project, neither realizes they are being filmed for a documentary. Over the course of their experience together, Bryan and Sabrina began to see each other in a new light, a sexual light. A bond between Bryan and Sabrina spills over at work. The project they're working on continues to get pushed back by their sexual episodes. Neither knows that a hidden camera is recording their thirst for each other. By the time they finished the project, the camera is revealed, and so is their sexual appetite for each other.

When I first wrote the script, I honestly had Amy on my mind. She was the ink behind my pen, the motivation. Initially, I wasn't aiming at her but it seemed like when she wasn't around, my head went blank. As soon as she appeared, the thoughts returned. I couldn't figure out what it was that drew me to her, what was it that as soon as she was in my presence, my mind expanded, knowledge came, stayed, like God gave me everything He said we weren't ready for.

It just didn't sit right with me, the way I craved her in such a way. She was my best friend's fiance, I was his best man. She was my secretary. Well, not like her being my secretary really mattered. But!

Everything that could go wrong with the session did. I couldn't pay my actors to remember a damn line from the script. And the sad thing, I was actually paying them. The more they messed up, the more I was ready to go to Brianna's house for dinner. Having sex in the company restroom would make a person think it would be a good day. It was the total opposite, like a bad omen.

As the day ended in Chaos, I sent everyone home early. I had to make the three-hour drive to Brianna's house, so I decided to get off early, to clear my head. It took me two and a half hours to get to her nice, ranch-style home. The house was sitting on at least an acre and a half. Her house was almost the same size as mine, not that she would ever see it to compare.

"Cupid!" Tristan yelled as he ran up to my truck like I was his father coming to take him fishing.

I stepped out of the truck with a smile on my face that I didn't try to hide. "Big guy, what's up?" I gave him a dap as I closed the door.

Briann stood at the front door behind the screen door, a beautiful smile on her face. Tristan led the way up the stairs. "You know I let you win that bet, right."

I laughed. "I'm glad you did, God only knows what I would've eaten if I hadn't won."

Brianna opened the door for us. "Hey, was it hard to find the house?" She asked as I walked inside. I pulled her close to me,

Moan in my Mouth

touching her lower back. The hug was much needed, and unexpected, on her behalf.

I looked at Tristian, he had a big kiddy smile on his face. "I'm sorry, I just had a," I sighed. "A difficult time at work today."

"Mind talking about it?" She asked.

"Over dinner, something smells great!" Brianna smiled.

"I didn't know what you would prefer, so I cooked a little of everything." She said as she led the way to the dining room.

I stared at her ass, the jeans she had on were tight, like she had to lie down to put them on.

"Did I tell you, you look amazing tonight?" I said, staring at her ass. Brianna looked over her shoulder and blushed, she knew exactly what I was getting at. As much effort she put into putting her tight jeans on, I had to show the effort of me noticing.

Tristan took his seat at the table, the very head. I applauded him for it, he was in fact the man of the house. I took my seat beside his, on the right side. Brianna came into the room with a plate full of food. I licked my lips as I looked at the plate.

Corn on the cob, greens, cornbread, fried chicken, macaroni and cheese, pinto beans, and broccoli and cheese. Everything looked so good I didn't know where to start. Brianna came back into her room with her plate, she took her seat and held her hand out to me, and Tristian. I held her hand, as well as Tristians.

It had been a while since I ate at a dinner table, even longer as of me praying over my food. My life was so busy, constantly moving, putting together scenes, and being a bachelor, I never took the time to consider the simple things of life; praying is one. The last time I prayed over my food was when I was at my dad's house for Christmas, which was two years ago. We had fallen out that day, for my own selfish reasons. He wanted me to settle down, give him some grandkids, knowing I wasn't trying to hear it. Why would I, when it took him forever to settle down?

"Cupid," Tristan said.

133

I opened my eyes, Tristians hand was still in mine, somehow Brianna had got hers back. "We said Amen, a minute ago," Tristan said laughing.

I shook my head as I picked my fork up. Brianna looked at me with care in her eyes. It was either that or fear that she let a maniac inside of her home. I dug into my food starting with macaroni and cheese. The taste was exquisite, the macaroni wasn't overcooked, the cheese was layered, half was shredded, the other half was Colby jack cheddar. My eyes had closed, once I opened them, Brianna was smiling, her fork being pulled from her lips.

"So, Cupid," Brianna said, breaking the silence. "Work really had you, distraught."

I nodded; then swallowed the food I had been savoring. "Today marks the first day in years my actors couldn't get a line right."

"Your actors? You're a producer, I didn't know that." She smiled.

"That explains the Rolex," Tristan said as cornbread crumbs fell from his mouth.

"Yes, I-I make, uhh, extreme movies." I looked at Brianna hoping she would get the hint.

"Extreme, like those extreme sports videos?" Tristan asked excitedly.

"I-uh, I guess you can say that, but we use a lot of balls." I kinda laughed at my own inside joke.

"Cool! Can we watch some?" Tristan asked.

I looked at Brianna, I didn't know how to explain myself without ruining the moment. Telling people what I did for a living was like passing gas at the dinner table while someone was praying.

"You have to be eighteen to watch them," I said, then looked at Brianna. "Have you talked to him about the birds and the bees?" She looked at me confused, then all of a sudden it hit her.

Brianna dropped her fork, the sound piercing the quiet moment. "What' the birds and the bees?" Tristan asked.

"The birds and the bees are-" I started to explain.

Moan in my Mouth

"Enough! Okay, Tristan, go eat your food in the living room, watch the game." Brianna said.

"But ma, you said to never eat in the living room while watching the game, that I'll turn out like all men, fat, and a bad husband."

I looked at Brianna and laughed. "Tristian go!" She spat.

Tristan grabbed his plate and cup of juice and left me to fend for myself, I had to teach him, Bro's before ... mothers.

"So, you're a -" Brianna said once Tristian was out of earshot.

"I own a professional porn company. I write and direct them, sell them, and the whole nine."

"Why didn't you tell me this in the beginning?" She asked as she gathered up our plates like we had finished eating.

"What was I supposed to say, hey, I'm Cupid. I think you're beautiful, you have a nice ass, and your son is super cool, by the way, I record people fucking for a living, very shitty job."

Brianna laughed which was a good sign, but I knew I wasn't out of the shit hole just yet. "You could've said something. I mean, 'I'm in the porn industry.' Would've helped."

"Professional," I said

"Huh?"

"We're professionals," I added.

Brianna threw her hands up defeated. "I really didn't think we would get this far. Normally I don't get a chance to explain what I do for a living, and when I do, no one really thinks too much of it."

Brianna shook her head as she carried the plates to the kitchen. I walked behind her, my mind on making things right, and getting my plate back. "I have a son, Cupid," she said as she sat both plates on the counter.

"And, what's that supposed to mean" I would think you would be happy I'm not a drug dealer. I don't have any kids, never been married, never had any STD and I said your kid was cool." She smiled.

"Be serious," she said smiling.

"Okay, serious." I inhaled, then exhaled. "You seriously took my plate," I said as I picked it up from the counter and bit into the chicken.

Brianna smiled and shook her head. "You're something else you know that." I picked the cornbread up and nodded.

"Mind if I catch the game with your cool ass son?" She smiled and fanned me away. I grabbed her chicken off her plate for good measure.

$$$

Chapter 22
-Trineka-

I agreed to accompany Cedrick on his trip to purchase a ring for the o-so lovely Amy. I only did it to spend more time with him. I just liked being around him. His vibe, his smile, personality, and spirit. His ambition, yes, that's what did it for me, his ambition. Cedrick was so talented it was unreal.

When Cedrick dropped his briefcase, I read some of his work. God, he was talented. His words were deep, passionate, and heartfelt. Fire was the way it felt as I read it. So, I agreed to go with him, but I told him he would have to go somewhere with me and he agreed.

As we walked inside the jewelry store, a Chinese woman walked up to us with a tray, two wine glasses sat on top filled with white wine. We accepted the glasses as we looked around. "Anything I can help you with, any specific cut, or stone you're looking for?" A man behind the counter asked. He was also Chinese, and he resembled the older lady that served us wine.

"I'm getting married, and I want to find the perfect ring for the perfect woman," Cedrick said.

" Well, you came to the right place. Our prices range from small deposits to large deposits, no credit, good, or bad credit. We have rubies, diamonds, pearls, you name it."

The man went off as he showed us a case of rings that looked like sparkling glass. "Show us the good diamonds," I said.

He took us to a different stand that had some beautiful rings in it. "Can I see that one?" I pointed.

"Nice choice," The salesman said as he unlocked the case and grabbed the heart-shaped ring. "This is a dome cut heart ring, it has twenty-four diamonds and twenty-six stones."

I pulled the diamond from its case and looked at it closely. It was beautiful. "You think she'll like it?" Cedrick asked.

I nodded, then looked at the ring case close to one back. "Can I see that one?" I asked as I handed the ring back.

The salesman replaced the ring and brought me the most beautiful ring I'd ever seen. "This is a Paris-styled cut. The center is a heart-shaped Ruby, 2.4 carats. The band and heart surrounding has twenty-eight surrounding diamonds, cut to perfection."

I nodded as he spoke to sell the ring. The ring was so beautiful; there was no need for a salesman; it can sell itself. I slid the ring on my finger, it fitted perfectly. I held it up, the sparkle that glistened from the diamonds made me want to buy it for myself.

"We'll take it," Cedrick said.

"Should I have it drawn up in payments?" The salesman asked.

Cedrick pulled out his black card and slid it across the counter. "Can we get a refill of what you served us, please?"

"Yes, my apologies." Cedrick nodded as the man spoke in a foreign language to the Chinese woman.

I pulled the ring off and handed it to Cedrick. "She's going to love it. She has to." I said on the verge of tears.

"Let's hope so, I saw the price tag, it cost me twelve thousand dollars," Cedrick said as the lady switched our glasses out with fresh ones.

"She's a very lucky woman. "I said as I took a sip from the wine. The first glass already had me feeling pretty relaxed.

"Jason will outdo me, I am sure of it."

I shook my head disgustingly at the mention of Jason's name. The bastard had yet to call me during his so-called 'business trip'. Yet he posted a million things on social media. I didn't let it get to me, I did what I've been doing since our relationship went public, dealt with it. I was used to it already, that's why it was time for me to start having my own fun; write my own chapters in the book called life.

"This isn't Jason's moment, it's yours. So, tell me how you're going to re-propose." I smiled as I took another sip of wine.

"I was just going to go home and show her," Cedrick said laughing.

"No, really." I shook my head, took a nice sip from the glass of wine, then sat it down. "You have to do it special. That's what

Moan in my Mouth

matters to us, the moments, the memories. How you did this or that. Not how much you spent." I stood up and said. "Hey, practice on me." I smiled.

"Right here, right now?" He asked with his glass in hand. I took the glass from him and sat it beside mine.

"You don't have any erasers in life, either you get it right, or you get it wrong. But, you can always prepare yourself, now's the chance."

Cedrick nodded. "You like putting me on the spot, huh." he laughed. "Okay." He said as he got down on one knee. He cleared his voice, grabbed my left hand in his and said.

"Amy, uhm. The day I first laid eyes on you, life seemed to slow down, the only thing that seemed to move fast was my heart. It wasn't so much as love at first sight, because I had love for you somehow before I ever laid eyes on you. It was like God sent a little bit of heaven down just for me. When I'm with you, every night is like the most precious stone, clear as crystal. When you walk, you make one ground look like gold. The angels from heaven look down on you with envy, the most sculptured masterpiece made from God's own hands. And yet you chose me. Luck has no comparison to how you make me feel. Blessed is only sugarcoating it. Loved, is only a portion and highly favored is just a nice way of saying it. God giving you to me was similar to Him sending Jesus down to die for our sins. It hurt him to send you down, but in the end, he knew it was for a great cause. So, I'm asking that you receive this ring, as a token, of forever. I'm not asking you to marry me. What I'm asking is if you ever decide to leave me, can I come too."

I nodded my head as tears streamed down my cheeks. Cedrick stood up, he wiped the tears from my eyes, such a perfect gentleman. "What did you think?" He asked me.

The Chinese woman sniffed from behind us." If she doesn't say yes, come back here, and I will." We both laughed.

***

Xtasy

-Cupid-

I was awoken by Brianna turning the TV off. My eyes opened, and I looked around. Tristan was nuzzled up under me, like father and son, he was knocked out, snoring. Brianna smiled, she had changed from her tight jeans into a pair of grey sweats, she still looked great, her figure still noticeable.

I eased up, careful not to wake the man of the house. Brianna did a motion with her hand, gesturing for me to pick Tristian up. I picked him up. The little bastard was heavy, full of his mother's chicken and macaroni. I kept his dirty little secret of him not eating his vegetables.

Brianna led the way through the house as I carried Tristian through the house. She opened his bedroom door, then pulled his covers back. I laid him down gently, then pulled the covers over him. I kissed his forehead and then walked off, he was really a cool kid. Brianna did the same, then followed me out of the room, closing the door quietly.

"I didn't even know I had fallen asleep until you had woken me up." I said as we made it to the living room.

"I know. I washed dishes, came to bring you two some dessert, and y'all were both snoring," she smiled.

"Me, snoring?" I played it off. "I was going to ask you, I hope he got his snoring from his dad."

Brianna playfully shoved me. "I don't snore." She smiled beautifully. I stared at her, not caring if it made her uncomfortable. I wanted her to see the way she made me feel. I was hoping, praying she could help me get Amy from my mind. I felt like Drake, I had two girls on my mind, and they're teens.

"Did you save me a piece of cake?" I asked, she only nodded and led the way to the kitchen. I didn't mind, the best view was from behind. A woman wasn't thick until she was thick in sweatpants.

Brianna pulled a piece of chocolate cake from the fridge, handed it to me, then a fork. "You made this too?" I asked as I cut a little piece away with the fork.

Moan in my Mouth

She nodded. "One of my favorite cakes, Devil's food." I nodded as I savored the sweet chocolate icing.
"You can throw down. This is amazing." I said as I took another bite.
She laughed. "What?" I asked as she pointed.
"You have-" She said walking up to me." Here, let me get it." She used her thumb as she wiped icing from the corner of my mouth. As she got it off, she smiled.
The cake in my hand no longer mattered, I had a new craving. I pulled her to me, my lips found hers, the taste of her lip gloss, strawberry. It went hand in hand with the devil's food. Damn devil!
As I pulled away, Brianna looked at me, then she slapped me. The initial shock is what shocked me. I didn't see it coming. The element of surprise. My hand went to where her hand just left. Before I could utter a word, she jumped on me like blood in a crip neighborhood. Her lips were on mine faster than people like a Kyle Jenner picture.
We bounced off the stove, then the counter then we fell to the floor. No talkin, just a bunch of spit boxing, tongue wrestling, liplocking. And she was an amazing kisser. I've always been able to do two things at once, but kissing, breathing, and trying not to moan took the cake. I had never moaned before, at least not on record, not that I would admit it if I had. But this woman, this white woman, made me almost moan. And by kissing.
She finally let me catch my breath. She lay under me, on the kitchen floor, panting, fire and desire in her eyes. "Brianna, I really think we should stop," I stopped briefly to catch my breath. "You don't know what you're getting yourself into."
She gave me a seductive smile. "Brianna, seriously, I'm trying to save you."
"From what," she asked. "I just want us to have a little fun. Simple, sex. That's it." She added.
I didn't know how to tell her she wasn't ready for what she was asking for. Maybe she felt that being with one black guy in bed was like being with all black guys. I knew this wasn't going to

141

end well. For one, I had a soft spot for her son. Then, I was really attracted to her.

Brianna pulled me back between her legs, the only thing standing between me punching her pussy like a baseball mitt was the inner me. I was a bachelor, not a loverboy. I liked her, her son too. If somehow she was to have some amazing, devil's food pussy, I knew I would be in big trouble. I wasn't ready to fall in love. Not admit it I mean.

OG wasn't making it easy for me. Sometimes I felt that I should put a collar on him, he was a dog in every sense. Brianna looked down below, her eyes told her I was packing more than clothes.

Brianna bit my bottom lip. She wasn't making this any easier for me. "We have to hurry, Tristan doesn't sleep long." Her shirt came over her head, her baby blue Victoria Secret bra was see-through, and my God, I could see through it.

I gave in, I couldn't help it. My nose found them first, then my hands. Her titties were soft, I played with them like it was my first time seeing a pair. She tossed her head back, her legs opened wider. I softly bit her brown nipples through the perfectly stitched fabric.

I shook my head, I had to see the rest of her, just in case the man of the house woke up. I kissed her at the same time I tugged at the waistband on her sweatpants. She lifted, giving me some assistance. Her bikini-cut panties matched her bra. Thank God for see-through panties and bras.

I leaned up on my knees and stared at her. I couldn't help but wonder why a man could abandon his son and the mother of his child. She was beyond beautiful. And her body, wham bam, thank you ma'am! As she watched me stare at her, she licked her lips. I leaned forward and cleaned up the spit she'd left behind.

I stood up, as did she. "On the counter, now," I demanded.

She looked at me, lust in her eyes. With her own strength, she hopped on the counter, I stood between her legs and she pulled my shirt over my head. She kissed my collarbone, her hands caressed my chest. I took a step back, I unbuckled my belt buckle, she

Moan in my Mouth

stared the entire time, I paused, then let my jeans fall to the floor. If anyone could say they knew Cupid, they would know I didn't wear briefs with jeans.

Brianna stared at OG, I picked him up and gently rubbed him to wake him fully. "This is OG, which is short for, oh God!" I introduced them properly. 'He loves to be stroked, softly though. He loves mouth baths, and he hates teeth. And with all due respect, don't choke him," I said smiling.

The more I stroked OG the more he stretched out. He began to curve as if he was trying to look back at me to see if he was really about to get the chance to have sex with the white woman in front of him. I laid my shirt on the ground and Brianna hopped off the counter. She turned her back to me, held her ponytail in her hand. I unhooked her bra, she let her hair go, and I kissed her back. She hooked her thumb in her panties and pulled them down slowly.

She faced the counter, naked, the cool breeze bringing goosebumps to her pale skin. I rubbed her perfect ass cheeks, warming them up. I kneeled behind her, like I was about to purpose to her beautiful pale ass. I bit her left cheek, I just wanted to see my teeth marks on her skin. I tapped her leg. She opened them, no words, just body language, sexology.

My finger moved between her sex lips, separating them, heat pouring from them like someone opened an oven. Pink was the only color I saw. Images of hubba bubba gum came to mind. I looked at her hubba bubba pussy, I just wanted to chew on it, savor the flavor, blow bubbles with it.

"You're going to play with your food, or are you going to eat it?" Brianna asked, looking over her shoulder.

I smiled, "Lay on my shirt, and remember, you asked for this." I scooted back on my knees to give her room.

I watched her as she lay on her back, on my shirt, keeping it so it wouldn't get misplaced. Her legs fell open, her pink gum showed, her wetness in the center, gusher. She sat up on her elbows, looking like a wet floor sign.

Xtasy

"Close your eyes," I said as I eased closer to her. She had a beautiful pussy. No bumps, no traces of hair, bikini wax. Nice, smooth, and bald, just like I liked it.

"No sounds, no moans, or you owe me another dinner. I want steak, eggs, and potatoes. Bet." I said. She smiled with her eyes closed and nodded.

I knew how to eat pussy. I loved doing it. I think OG liked fucking more, and I loved eating them alive. I was so good, I could teach a class on it. It was just something about it, the way it tasted, sweet and salty. I always started around the pussy, the sensitive spots, the mound, the inner thigh. It's what gets the faucet dripping.

I kissed her mound and brushed my lips over it, no feel of hair on her end, I knew she could feel the hair under my bottom lip, the hair I grew on purpose, the clit tickler. Her body squirmed, but no sounds came, she had discipline.

I stood up, she opened her eyes. "No cheating, keep them closed." She closed them back with a smile on her face. I opened the fridge and scanned the contents until I found what I was looking for. I closed the fridge back, a handful of grapes in my hand.

I kneeled before her most prized possession, the baby maker, where the man of the house came from. I popped a grape in my mouth and chewed it, to make sure they were seedless. I put another in my mouth, centered my mouth with her hole, then spat the grape deep inside her hole. She flinched, ginned, but kept quiet. I repeated the process, putting another tasteful grape in her hole. After the second grape, I let them stay there, marinate. By the time I went back for them, I wanted them to be soaked, mixed with grape juice, and pussy juice.

I closed my eyes, that is what makes eating pussy so special. Hers closed, mine too, both of us imagining fantasies of each other. I kneeled over her like an altar, my eyes closed as if I was praying. I kneeled closer, my mouth opened, tongue wet with anticipation, grape juice. I licked her sex lips, paid my tithes.

Moan in my Mouth

I used my fingers to open her sex lips, my elbow holding her legs open. I laid my face on her thigh, and licked her clit from the side like Ray J did Kim K. Brianna's body moved, her toes curled, but no sound. Damn her discipline! I inched my index finger and middle finger inside her hole, the tip of my fingers touching the grapes checking to see if they were ready. Brianna started grinding on my fingers, her eyes still closed, lips tight, grunts, but no words.

I pulled my fingers out. Pulled the hood that covered her clit apart. Her pearl glistened, I blew on it, my warm breath caused it to stand out, she squirmed, grunted louder. I licked her pearl, swiped it like it was an ice cream cone. I closed my warm lips around her pearl, clamped down on it, hummed, sung the national anthem, Snoop Dogg's version, sexual seduction.

That got a sound from her. "Uh-uhh!" She moaned as her back raised off the ground, possessed as I spoke in tongues on her clit.

I flicked my tongue faster, images of her cake, the icing, devils food. Images of the spoon she used, I licked it clean, devil's food. My stomach growled, it was time. My tongue swam inside her hole, swimming as far as it could go.

"Ahh-fuck!" She gave in. "God, Cupid, please!" She moaned as my tongue hooked inside of her to try to get the grape that had swelled with her juices. I worked my tongue, fished it around, pulled the grape with my tongue and held it in my mouth as I hoovered over her mouth. I kissed her, her tongue moved in my mouth, tasting her juices, the grape, devil's food. I broke the kiss, the grape was no longer in my mouth, her jaws moved, she chewed the grape, a thief, devil.

I went back for round two, I left something. I moved my tongue inside her hole her ass eased off the ground, off my shirt, my tongue with it, lodged inside her hole. The tip of my tongue touched the grape, it was farther than the last.

"Ahh, fuck Cupid! Wh-what are you doing, uhm fuck, that feels so damn good." She said as her eyes opened fully.

I gripped her pale thighs, pulled them closer to me, I was determined to get the grape, I never give up on any task. I massaged

Xtasy

her ass cheeks as I sunk my tongue deeper. My tongue hooked the grape, a smile came to my face. I slowly pulled the grape out, it was fat and juicy. I held it with my tongue, Brianna stared at me, amazed at the trick. I showed her the grape on my tongue, then I chewed it, eyes closed, savored the flavor, devil's food.

I grabbed a hold of OG, he had waited in patience. I shook him, white creme came from his mouth, like I had burped him. I swiped the precum from OG and rubbed it between my thumb and pointer finger. I neared OG at her entrance, the sight was beautiful, it could've been said pay-per-view.

I massaged her clit with the crown of OG, her body squirmed. "Ss-ss, God, don't tease me," she moaned as she spread her legs wider.

I placed OG at her center, pushed the head in, breaking through her safe zone, she moaned, arched her back and bit her bottom lip. I leaned my head to hers, our foreheads touched, she wrapped her left arm around my neck OG inched inside of her.

"I feel it," she moaned. "Oooh, I feel it," she said.

I kissed her, trying my hardest not to moan. The feeling of her pussy, her warmth, the wetness, the grip it had on OG. OG moved deeper, I moved my hips, she kissed my lips, a tear escaped her eye, we moved in unison, the perfect tango. I moved my hips faster, I closed my eyes and squeezed them tight; her pussy was the bomb. I shook my head, her hand went to my left ass cheek, she gripped it, pulled me closer, deeper.

I opened my eyes, she was looking at me, tears falling down her cheeks, her mouth opened, she moaned. "Deeper," she said. I nodded, wanting to, but afraid that if I went deeper, her pussy would get better and better, like it had different levels.

I gave her what she asked for, and got what I feared in return. I went deeper, her pussy tightened, squeezed and clamped around OG. My mouth opened, I hovered over her lips, she kissed my open mouth, our hips moved at the same time.

"Uhhm, fuck Cupid," she moaned. "Let it out, babe. It's okay, it's okay. Moan in my mouth, it's okay."

Moan in my Mouth

I shook my head, I couldn't, I wouldn't. I was a bachelor, I just couldn't. Brianna squeezed her vaginal muscles, I felt it, OG did too. The feeling was amazing. She felt it too, her mouth opened, as did mine, then I did the unthinkable, the forbidden. I moaned.

"Ohh, uhhh," I moaned in her mouth, at the same time OG burped again, this time inside of her. I pulled out, Brianna quickly turned over, positioned herself on her knees, ass in the air. I stroked OG, fast, he spat all over her juicy ass, she wiggled it, teasing me. My body shook, OG kept spitting up, target practice on her juicy ass.

He finished, and I fell backwards on my knees. I rubbed my cum in her ass cheeks, smacked them, then kissed them. She turned around and kissed me, our kiss broke, our eyes locked, a sharp tingle passed through my heart. I knew at that moment that I'd been shot, damn Cupid and his arrows.

$$$

Xtasy

Chapter 23
-Cedrick-

After I and Trineka grabbed Amy a ring, I let her take me into going with her to a place she said was filled with a lot of great talent. She drove, and the entire time, she made me keep my eyes closed. I kept trying to peek during the ride, yes she would catch me every time. It became a game for us, and before we knew it, we had reached our destination.

"We're here," she said as the truck stopped. I opened my eyes and looked around.

We were parked in front of a small red brick building called, 'Lyfe's pain'. "What is it?" I asked. She smiled and took the keys from the ignition.

"You'll have to come inside and see for yourself." She stepped out of the truck. I took my seatbelt off and stepped out following behind her.

Trineka walked inside first and I followed behind her. The inside was dark, barely lit. Small round tables filled the room, a few booths surrounded the walls. A large bar was in the back, the bartender is a Caucasian woman with black hair. A stage was to the front of the room, a mic in the center, a wooden stool behind it.

"Be right back," Trineka said as she walked off to talk to the bartender. I nodded and continued to look around. The place wasn't packed, but there was a nice crowd present.

"We're table number ten," Trineka said as she walked up to me. She led the way to our circle table." This place is my place of peace. The bartender is a very good friend of mine, her name is Lyfe. We went to college together."

"So, what is this place? I see the mic, and the stool."

"Look, you'll find out now."

I looked as a Caucasian male with blonde dreads took the stage. He sat on the stool, adjusted the mic and cleared his throat. "Good evening ladies and gents', my name is Ralphie, and this poem is entitled, 'Emotionally unstable'."

I looked at Trineka, she smiled at me. I looked back to the stage as Ralphie began.

"Fuck life, that was I, that was me, yea I said it! I have no purpose, no drive, and no reason to say I regret it!

Fuck people, so judgemental, but walk around with their heads in their asses; they can't see where they're headed. I hate their comments, I hate their existence, it bothers me and I don't know why I let it.

Fuck twelve, the police, who are you to tell me what I can't do? How I'm feeling right now, I'll kill your whole family, burn your house down and leave a note explaining why I can't stand you.

Fuck ethnicity, we all bleed, hurt, and have problems we might not handle. But that's no reason to judge a man by the color of his skin or because the texture his hair gives him a different hairdo.

Fuck birds, and their wings. My, don't they think they're splendid. Tomorrow I might try to be a bird, climb to the highest peak and take flight. Sucks my life never started before contemplating how to end it.

So fuck life, that was I, that was me, yea I said it. I'm emotionally unstable in desperate need of help. If I can't get it, then fuck it, I already know where I'm headed."

After he finished, the room erupted in snaps. Ralphie stood up and walked off the stage. I smiled, a gush of air left my lungs. "That was heartfelt," I said to Trineka.

"Wait until you hear the next act." She said. I looked around, there was a spotlight moving across the room, everyone waited to see who it would land on.

Then it landed on me. I looked at Trineka, she smiled, I shook my head. "Don't be scared, they'll love you, just say it." She encouraged.

I took a sip from the drink that sat in front of me. I hope that it gave me courage. I stood up, all eyes were on me as I walked to the stage. I walked up the steps, walked behind the mic and took a seat on the wooden stool. I adjusted the mic to reach my face, then I cleared my throat.

"My name is Cedrick. This is my first time, so please bear with me. This is entitled, 'my strange reality'." I cleared my throat again and began.

"Left foot, right foot, left foot, right. A constant rhythm I keep as I stumble through life.

Head heavy as boulders hanging low as my shoulders. I don't appear in the day as I appear at night.

A known fuck up my parents and teachers would say the same. I'm the outcast, the black sheep, my presence, the reason it rains.

My mom says I'm the devil, and my dad says I need change. I know I'm possessed by demons because my reflection looks at me strange.

My head has voiced, and my shadows have shadows. My head says let's go drown in a lake and influence everyone else to follow.

Or maybe climb three hundred feet and jump headfirst in a stream that's shallow. In the day, my life is a nightmare on Elm Street, and at night, the legend of sleepy hollow.

I might just follow you home, tie you up and drag you to the dead end. Your pain is my pleasure, so excuse me while I enjoy contemplating smashing your head in.

Ouija board, ouija board can I talk to my dead friend? I've called the wrong spirit now, this evil game will never end.

Right foot, left foot, right foot, left. A constant rhythm I keep as I evade arrest. I broke into a house and shot the owner in the chest. He prayed for me to be captured, as I prayed for his last breath.

My heart is rapidly beating, and my palms are filled with sweat. Sometimes I wish life was a dream, so who'd fuckin' cares what happens next. But that's just my estranged reality."

I stood up, the room erupted with snaps. I smiled and walked off the stage. Trineka stood up with her arms wide as I walked back to our table. I walked into her embrace, she smelt good as her scent ran through my nose.

"That was deep, scary almost. I could see what you were saying, almost like you were painting the picture right before my eyes. The way you spoke, it was like you had experienced it all." She said.

"I wasn't always the head of A&R."

***

-Amy-

I come home to find the house empty. This was the first time I beat Cedrick home since I've been working. I usually came home and Cedrick would already have the house clean and dinner ready.

As I was in the bedroom cleaning up, Cedrick came home. I heard him drop his keys on the tray by the door, then he stumbled into the room. "Hey," he greeted me.

"Hi," I replied. I looked at him, he looked tired, his eyes glossy.

"How was work?" he asked as he sat his briefcase on the floor. He unbuttoned his shirt and tossed it on the floor, ignoring the fact that I was cleaning up.

"It was okay, I guess. And yours?"

"Pretty good." He said then looked at me. "Amy, about last night."

"Uh, huh."

"I'm sorry. I shouldn't have let her kiss my cheek, especially not on camera." He said. I looked at him, his voice was shaky, slurred, like he had been drinking.

"It's okay, I'm past that." I stepped closer to him, he hugged me and kissed my forehead, then lips. His breath smelled like wine, his shirt had a funny fragrance to it, a perfume smell.

Cedrick pulled away. 'I need to take a shower, then we'll talk more," I nodded. I couldn't get past the smell of his breath and the perfume smell.

Moan in my Mouth

Cedrick walked to the bathroom, he left the door open as he turned the shower on, my suspicion got the best of me. "Where'd you go after work?"

"Uhm, I came straight home, why?" He asked as he stepped into the shower.

"I just asked, no reason," I said as I sat on the edge of the bed. I looked to the floor beside me, his briefcase sat there. I picked it up, sat it across my lap and silently clicked the locks, it popped open.

Inside were a stack of papers, a few files, his iPhone, a pack of gum, his phone charger, and his custom pens with his name on them. I looked to the bathroom, the shower curtain was closed. I picked his phone up, and balanced the briefcase with my knees. I didn't have to go through a sequence of numbers, his phone wasn't locked.

I scrolled through his text messages, Cedrick had a new unread text from a name, Trineka. I opened the message, it read.

: Had an awesome time with you tonight. You really convinced me you have a way with words. They were stronger than your hands, more passionate than anything I've ever heard. I really wanted you to go another round, but I knew you had drunk too much wine. But, I just wanted you to know I love the pain, I felt it, when you released it, I knew it came from deep down. Thank you for the amazing night, I'll never forget it.

I didn't know I had started crying until the tears landed on the screen. I couldn't believe him, fuckin' lier, cheater! I know I was no different, me having thoughts of doing sexual favors with Cupid, his best friend, best man. But those were only thoughts, nothing more. But him, Ced, oh my God, he cheated. He fuckin' cheated.

I stood up, his phone in hand. I wasn't the bitch to be cheated on. I wasn't! I walked to our closet, it was full of all his tailored and high price suits. I began to yank them down, threw them into a pile on the floor. I walked out of the hall closet, grabbed a bottle of bleach and walked back to the bedroom. I twisted the cap, tossed it to the other side of the room, wasn't any need of keeping track of it, I was using this whole bottle.

I tilted the bottle, then I turned it upside down, not caring what it got on. The smell was strong, potent in the air.

"Damn babe, what you in there spring cleaning?" Cedrick said from the shower as the strong odor reached the bathroom. I closed my eyes tight at hearing his voice.

I had had enough. I stormed into the bathroom, yanked the curtain back. He jumped, like he had been doing something he had no business doing. Cedrick washed the soap from his face. He was smiling, as if he thought I would join him. That was until he saw the look on my face and his phone in my left hand.

"Amy, what's wrong?" He asked as the water cascaded down his body. He looked at the seriousness on my face, the way I held his phone, ready to throw it at him.

"I asked you where you went after work, you lied and said straight home. Who's Trineka?" I asked. I closed my eyes and shook my head. "Please tell me that's not the same bitch that kissed you on video." He didn't answer me, which made me madder. "Is it?" I yelled.

"Amy," he said softly, reaching out the shower to me. His eyes sobered up, care was in them, yet I no longer cared.

"I can't believe you, you-you, cheater!" I threw his phone at his head, his quick reflexes made him move his head, but I still managed to graze the side of his head.

"Dammit, Amy!" He yelled as he grabbed the side of his head, he pulled his hand from his head, blood was on it.

"I want you out of my house! Fuck the couch, fuck the man cave, I want you out!" I walked out of the bathroom before he could get a chance to get out of the shower.

"Amy, talk to me, you never give me a chance to explain anything."

"What is there to explain, you lied to my face. Fro no fuckin' reason! Liar!" I spat.

"Who says I'm lying?" He asked.

"I saw the fuckin' messages on your phone, so don't try that shit with me!"

"What are you doing going through my phone," he said then shook his head. "Trineka said you didn't trust me, and she was right. You're snooping through my shit, why?"

Because I cant' fuckin trust you!" I yelled.

"If you can't trust me, then why are you with me, huh?"

I sat quietly at his question. I had asked myself how can a man say he loves his woman, his fiance, and yet he lies to her, cheats and acts like it's nothing. "That's a good question," I said. I grabbed my phone and car keys. "Since you won't leave, I will."

$$$

Xtasy

Chapter 24
-Trineka-

Last night was yet another lonely night in my bed. A bed I shared with Jason, my so-called fiance. As I was lying in bed last night, I received a text from a random number. It was a picture, with no words. The picture was of Jason, he was asleep in bed, he didn't have his ring on. I was no fool, I knew it could only be Brandi texting me from another number, childish ass bitch, or bitches, because it could be one of the other whore I knew Jason had behind my back.

See, what Brandi thought she was doing, was taking Jason away from me. But how could you take something from someone when they didn't care to keep it. Brandi was clueless though, she didn't know, she wasn't working hard for the main bitch spot, she was working hard for the main side bitch spot. Dumbass tramp!

I sat behind my desk as I relieved the evening I shared with Cedrick the night before. He was so smart, so talented, and articulate. He was the man of my dreams, my fantasy. God, how I wished I had met him before I'd met Jason; before Cedrick became engaged.

A light double knock came at my office door. "Come in!" Cedrick walked inside, a smile came to my face. "Good-" I started to say. The look on his face looked as if he hadn't had a good morning. I stood up, "Cedrick, are you okay?" I asked, concerned.

He walked up to me. "You were right." He said.

"About what?" I asked.

"She doesn't trust me, at all. She went through my phone, my briefcase. She suspects me of cheating. She saw your text." He explained.

My hand went to my mouth, "Oh, Cedrick. I'm so sorry." I walked closer to him. The strong smell of liquor explained his look.

Cedrick grabbed my arm. He pulled me closer to him, his lips found mine, my eyes closed, mouth opened. I gasped, fought his tongue to get the last bit of breath. My pussy got wet, his hand

Xtasy

went to my ass, he gripped it. I broke our kiss, as much as I wanted it, wanted him, he was drunk.

I huffed to catch my breath. "Cedrick, what was that about?" I asked, blushing.

"I wanted to see something. I wanted to see if you could make my heart flutter like Amy does."

My smile faded, but I had to ask, my pride got the best of me. "So, what did you feel?" I asked.

"Nothing. Not a flutter, or a skip. No fire, no erection, nothing. I thought it would be something because you're beyond beautiful, but it wasn't. And I'm sorry, I really am." He backed away, turned and left. Bastard, didn't even stay to see the tears fall down my cheeks.

***

-Cupid-

"No! That's not how I want it done!" I shouted at my crew as they failed to do the scene correctly, again.

"You know what, take five," I said, then shook my head. "You know what take thirty!" I said irritability.

I sat on my director's chair as everyone filed out of the room. The AFVs were months away. I would have to get the project done by next month to get a good buzz from it, and people would have to like it.

I shook my head as Amy stood beside me. "Do you need anything?" She asked.

I stood up, grabbed a script, and said. "I need for them to do exactly what I'm paying them to do. I mean, how fuckin' hard could it be." I grabbed the remote to the sound system and turned it up, imagining I was a part of the movie. I closed my eyes, opened them and began to recite a line from the script.

"I loved working with you. And in the process of working with you, I fell in love with you."

Moan in my Mouth

Amy walked up to me, another script was in her hands. "In the beginning, I didn't understand the point of the project, picking us two to do a job we're way advanced for. Then over the course of these past few weeks, I realized that this job wasn't a task, it was a test."

"A test of love," we said in unison. Amy took a step closer to me as Giveons' For Tonight started playing in the background.

"We've been done
Long before it all began
Still can't give it up
Lead me on
But leave before the morning comes
Even though it's what we want
Can't keep this up for long-"

I stared into Amy's eyes. I looked so deep that I could see myself in them. She stood before me, stuck, the script held at her side, waiting for me to do as the script read next, which was to kiss her. I stepped closer, the script held tightly in my hand. Giveon singing about the way I was feeling, what I was thinking, setting the mood.

"'Cause all I wanna do is lie with you
We've become numb to what we know is wrong
But no one knows but us
The feelings rush every single time we touch-"

I placed my mouth close to hers, I hesitated she moved her lips closer to mine. Our lips touched and the script fell from my hand to the floor. My eyes closed, her lips tasted sweet, devil's food.

***

-Cedrick-

After leaving Trineka's office, I had to get out of there. I lied to her face, for no reason. I told her that I felt nothing from the kiss. That my heart didn't even skip a beat. Yet it was all a lie, a

bold-face lie. The kiss did make my heart flutter, in fact, it skipped like a scratched-up CD.
 The reason I lied to her was that I was afraid. I was engaged. Yet I had feelings for my boss' wife, and I knew she had feelings for me too. She was truly beautiful, skin deep. Her heart was big, she cared for me. I knew that the first day I met her. A woman's eyes are a dead give-away. I thought she was an amazing woman, there was no doubt in that but I was engaged. I couldn't let my fiance just give up on us, and I just couldn't sit back and not fight for her. God knows she was worth fighting for.
 I stopped by the liquor store and snatched up another bottle of Hennessy. As I got back in my G-Wagon, I tossed my ID inside the glove department. Before closing it back, I looked at the .44 Magnum that I had tucked inside for safekeeping.
 I peeled the cap on the Hennessy and took a nice gulp. The liquor wasn't to quince my thirst, it was to ease the ache I felt inside. I pulled off and drove a few blocks to Cupid's place of business, 'Pandora's Poison'. I had to see Amy, I just had to. I wanted to hold her, feel her heartbeat, and tell her how much I love her.
 I pulled up to Pandora's Poison and parked right beside Amy's Porsche. I took another gulp from the Hennessey, then another for good measure. I tossed the bottle in the passenger seat, grabbed a mint from the cup holder, then stepped out in the hot sun. I placed my sunglasses over my eyes as I walked up to the building.
 "Welcome to Pandora's Poison," The doorman said with a huge smile on his face.
 "You must be Chad?" I surprised him by saying his name.
 "How'd you know?" Chad asked, surprised.
 "My wife Amy talks about you. She says you're the best doorman in all of Texas." I laid it on thick but she did mention him once.
 "Amy's your wife? She's amazing."
 "Do you know where she's at?" I asked.

"Um, she might be at her desk, which is all the way to the right. Or, she might be in studio one,"

I nodded. "Thank you, Chad. Keep up the good work." I applauded him as he held the door open for me.

I walked inside, the place looked bigger than it did on the outside. Men and women dressed professionally walked back and forth up and down the hallways. I looked to the right the direction Chad gave me to find Amy. I walked down the hall in search of her.

I wanted to surprise her. Show her I was willing to fight for her. Isn't that what women want, to be fought for? I hope she did, because I wasn't leaving without a fight.

I walked to her desk, there was a sign that sat on her desk that read: studio one. I looked around until I could find someone to assist me. "Excuse me, miss. Could you assist me in finding studio one?"

The Caucasian woman smiled. "Yes, take any of those two elevators, press studio one. The whole floor is studio one."

"Thank you," I said as I walked off. I waited on the elevator with very little patience. As the elevator opened, I rushed inside and pressed studio one. As the doors closed, I silently prayed that Amy would forgive me.

***

The elevator door opened. There was no one walking around like it was on the first floor. I looked around, Cupid really had it going on here. I noticed when I was in the elevator that he had another Studio on the third floor. I had to congratulate him after I and Amy swept everything under the rug.

I heard music from a distance, I followed the sound.
"Can't keep this up for long
But I just, I just don't wanna leave you
Might just, might just throw away the reasons why
 We both can't lay here
And secret, secret, both gotta keep it

Honest, honest, that's just a game we know (know)
We both can't play -"

I bobbed my head to the song as I looked around for Amy. The sign on her desk read that she was up here. I walked all the way inside the room, the music got louder.

"So deny the truth
We'll stay behind closed doors -"

I heard a faint moan close by. I looked around, there was a small fake office setup. A desk, chair, couch, and a bunch of other office supplies. I heard more moans, this time stronger than before. I walked closer to the set. The moans came this time with words.

"Fuck, you're so deep!" A female voice moaned. I looked around, wondering if this was part of a movie scene.

"Uh! Fuck! Damn, right there!" The voice got louder and more familiar.

The background music started over, like it was on repeat.

"We've been done
Long before it all began
Still can't give it up
Lead me on
But leave before the morning comes-"

I walked closer to the couch, the smell of sex flooded my nose. "Harder daddy, I'm so wet, harder!" The familiar voice moaned. I knew I had drunk a little, oh, who was I kidding. I knew I was drunk, but the more the woman moaned the more her voice sounded like Amy.

A hand fell over the back of the couch, it was the woman's. I could tell by how her hands looked. And how big her diamond ring was. The diamond ring almost looked exactly like Amy's. In fact, it looked exactly like hers.

"Cum in me, cum in me Cupid!" The familiar voice said. I shook my head, it had to be the Hen' dog talking to me. I walked closer to the couch, close enough to where I could see over it. I noticed Cupid, he was power driving the woman under him. I couldn't see his companion's face because his head was in the way.

As Cupid went deeper, Amy's head fell backwards, her mouth opened, yet no words came out. Wait, did I just say, Amy.

"Amy!" I shouted, her eyes opened, looked right at me.

Cupid tried to look over his shoulder, I snatched him up and tossed him on the floor. Amy sat up and covered herself like I hadn't seen her naked before. I jumped over the couch like a cop does the hood of a car.

"My wife!" I punched Cupid in the mouth. "My fuckin' wife!" I punched him again.

"Ced, stop!" Amy screamed.

I kept punching Cupid like he was a total stranger; like we hadn't grown up together; like I didn't name him my best man. I looked down at his dick, I got more upset, his dick was bigger than mine. I punched the shit out of him, hard. Blood spewed out of his nose, his mouth was bloodied. Amy jumped on my back to get me off of Cupid. I slung her over my shoulders. I wasn't trying to hurt her, the liquor mixed with my anger put me in a rage.

I let up off of Cupid, temporarily. I grabbed a light stand that resembled a microphone stand. I held it over my head, I stared at Cupid, his eyes barely open. He saw me, he grunted, tried to get out of the way.

"C-Ce-Ced', I'm, so-rry!" he said. A single tear fell from my eye.

I shook my head. I should've known better. Cupid had always been a man whore. He never cared who's woman he fucked. I should've seen it coming.

"C-Ced', please!" Cupid said.

I shook my head, closed my eyes, and brought the light stand down with all my strength. I opened my eyes, Cupid lay completely still on the floor, blood was all over my shoes and the weapon. People gasped behind me, I looked to see a crowd of spectators, witnesses to my crime. I dropped the weapon, looked around, I spotted Amy getting up off the floor, she was still naked from the waist down. People had their phones out, recording me.

Xtasy

I ran, fled. I had to get away, I had to. I came to apologize to get my queen back; to tell her how much of a fool I was, and how I would do anything to get her back. Instead, I find my fiance, and my best friend having sex, fucking, or however they want to clarify it. An entanglement.

I ran to my G-Wagon, a crowd had followed me outside, their cameras still rolling. I opened the passenger door, opened the glove compartment, and grabbed my gun. I was only planning on scaring the fake camera crew off. Someone grabbed my arm, I turned, at the same time, I was raising my gun, it went off. The shot was loud, and people scrambled, but not before Amy's body could hit the pavement.

I looked at her, she was shaking, blood poured from a small hole in her neck. I fell to my knees beside her, I placed her hand over the gunshot wound. I scooped her up, she was light, I opened the backdoor and carefully placed her in the backseat and kissed her forehead.

"It's going to be okay, I'ma get you to a hospital," I said as I closed the door. I ran around to the driver's seat, opened the door and jumped inside. I looked to the backseat, she was still breathing.

I turned the key and drove off, the gun in my hand. "Amy, stay awake babe, please!" I said as I kept looking to the backseat.

I sped through traffic, switching lanes as I heard police sirens in the distance. I looked in my rearview mirror, Amy was still breathing, but the blue blood was gaining on me. I turned right as fast as I could, I avoided hitting a parked car, and as I sped through a red light, the police did the same.

I looked to the backseat, Amy was coughing up blood. "Stay awaked, we're almost there babe!" Police cars were coming at me from all directions, I even heard a helicopter over my head. I looked around and noticed there weren't too many cars in the streets anymore. It was just my G-Wagon leading the race with at least twenty police cars behind me, and the blue bird flying over my head.

Moan in my Mouth

I saw the hospital up ahead. "We're close babe," I said as I let my feet squeeze the pedal to the floor. Smoke came from under the hood as I drove as fast as the engine would allow. I drove into the emergency room parking lot, parked and looked to the back seat. Amy's eyes were open, glossy, and lifeless. Her hand was hanging, her mouth covered in blood.

"N-No! Amy!" I cried as I climbed into the backseat. I lifted Amy to my lap. Her eyes didn't blink, no air came from her lungs. I held her, cried and kissed her bloodied lips.

"I'm so sorry babe." I cried as my forehead rested on hers. Please forgive me. Look, I'm not mad anymore, I forgive you." I looked to the front seat, my briefcase.

"Wait right here, I have something for you. I almost forgot." I gently laid her head down and climbed into the front seat. Police surrounded the G-Wagon but at a safe distance. I heard someone yelling into a bullhorn.

I grabbed the bottle of Hennessy, my briefcase, and climbed back in the backseat. "Look what I got you," I said as I unlocked the locks on my briefcase. I pulled the ring out and tossed the briefcase on the floor. I held the box and held it out to her. I pulled the ring from the box, then tossed the box to the floor.

I pulled the engagement ring from her ring finger, then eased the wedding ring I'd bought on her ring finger. I held her hand up, "look how good it looks on you babe" I said as tears streamed down my face.

I grabbed the Hennessy bottle and twisted the cap. "We have to celebrate now," I said as I took the bottle to the head. I held Amy's head up and poured some into her mouth. Instead of it going down her throat, it came out the corners of her mouth. Tears continued to fall, and a man's voice demanded I turn the engine off and release the hostage. Amy wasn't a hostage, she was my wife. We just got married, they just didn't see the ring I put on her finger.

I kissed Amy's lips again. I looked out the back window, there was a news van parked behind a yellow caution tape, they were recording me. I climbed into the front seat, Hennessy bottle

165

Xtasy

in my hand. I sat in the driver's seat, and turned the radio up to drown out the bull horn behind me. I twisted the cap, grabbed my gun and sat it on my lap. I took the bottle to the head as Chris Stapleton sang from down deep.

> "Girl, the way you broke my heart
> It shattered like a rock through a window ...
> I thought we had it so good
> Never really saw this comin' ...
>
> Oh, why you got to be so cold?
> Why you got to go and cut me like a knife
> And put our love on ice?
>
> Oh, girl you know you left this hole
> Right here in the middle of my soul
> Oh, why you got to be so cold?"

I looked through the rearview mirror, I guess the police were tired of negotiating, they decided to come and get me. As they snuck up beside a bunch of parked cars, I grabbed my gun from my lap. I pointed it at my head. I looked through the rearview mirror, tears fell from my eyes, my lips began to shake, I stared at Amy.
"I love you, Mrs. Montgomery."
Bang!

$$$

Chapter 25
-Trineka-

The entire Bloody Lyrics staff watched Cedrick's high-speed chase live in the boardroom. That's everyone except Brandi and Jason. Jason was too busy trying to hide Brandi's new pregnancy. Brandi flaunted it on Facebook for the world to see. I cried, only for a moment. That was until Belofante came to get me.

As I walked into the boardroom, everyone was standing around the large flat screen TV in shock. I squeezed my way through to see what all the chaos was about. Once I saw the TV, I read the headline and covered my mouth with my hand.

: Bloody Lyric record A&R director assaulted a man at his own business and kidnaps woman.

I shook my head as a picture of Amy popped up on the screen. She was exactly as he had described her. Beautiful.

"A high-speed chase has been going on for just a couple of miles. The driver, who police believe to be, a Mr. Cedrick Montgomery went by a porn industry known as Pandora Poison. Witnesses claim to have heard yelling, then some witnessed Mr. Montgomery assaulting the owner, Mr. Cupid Patterson with a light stand. As witnesses pulled out their phones to record, Mr. Montgomery fled to his SUV, where more witnesses witnessed him shoot Ms. Amy Nyugen, who people claim is Mr. Montgomery's fiance. Witnesses later claim Mr. Montgomery carried Ms. Nyugen to his SUV and fled. The police have been tailing him ever since." The news reporter said as the camera went back to Cedrick's G-Wagon.

I wiped the tears from my eyes as I watched him swerve in and out of lanes. I just didn't understand it, I couldn't comprehend what was going on. Cedrick was just here, he was just in my office. The kiss, the feel of his lips against mine, his strong hands against my ass. He was here, making a difference, motivating everyone to be greater. Now he was on television, running from the police, a high-speed chase.

Xtasy

I looked at the TV, we all did. Everyone watched as Cedrick pulled into the hospital lot. He parked, the police parked close by, sealing the exits with a barricade of police cars. People walked out of the hospital, saw what was going on, then ran back inside.

I could only imagine what was going on inside of Cedrick's head. I cried, thinking it was all my fault. I was to blame. I was so into him, his swag, his demeanor, his personality, I didn't care about his ring finger, his own marriage. I talked down on Brandi, on Jason, yet I was just like them. Inconsiderate of what others felt. I was the one who planted the seed, put the thought in his head that she didn't trust him. Then I sent a text to his phone, a mixed message. My plan worked, Amy found it, she badgered him, even went out her way to say we were cheating. Exactly what I made the message look like. I got what I wanted, but was it worth it?

"Look!" Belofante pointed at the TV. "Looks like they're about to go get him."

I looked closer at the TV as four police officers snuck past a parked car to get closer to Cedrick's G-Wagon. I wanted to scream, yell for him to watch out, yet I knew he wouldn't be able to hear me. As the officers got closer to the car, the news station got quiet, everyone in the room went silent; everyone anticipating what was to come. A loud gunshot sounded and a flash sparked inside Cedrick's SUV. The officers that were sneaking up took off for cover. About twenty seconds passed before they abandoned their cover. They crept on both sides of Cedrick's G-Wagon. They had their assault rifles aimed at the truck. The camera crew went around to the driver's side for a better view. An officer opened the driver's side door and Cedrick's body fell out of the truck and hit the ground hard, the gun at his side for the whole world to see.

More officers walked up, a gurney was brought out of the hospital and Amy's body was placed on it. They performed some quick tests, but I could look at her and see she wasn't coming back.

"We are showing you live footage, the suspect, Cedrick Montgomery has been presumed dead, a fatal, self-inflicted gunshot to the head. As you can see, nurses and doctors are checking for a pulse on Ms. Nyugen-. I-I just received some terrible news, word just came in that Ms. Amy Nyugen has been pronounced dead. This has been just a horrible day in DFW."

I wiped my eyes and walked off. Tears continued to stream down my face. I walked past my office to Cedricks. I unlocked the door, his cologne scent still lingered in the air. I walked off to Jason's office, unlocked the door, and walked inside. I went around to his drawer, opened it and pulled out his gun. I closed the drawer back and left, leaving the door wide open.

I walked to the studio, the same one I and Cedrick sat in to record Belofante's new number one single. I closed the door behind me and locked it. I walked inside the soundproof room and closed the door. I sat on the stool, the microphone stand was in front of me. I went to my videos on my phone and clicked on Belo's studio recording.

I cocked Jason's gun, held it in my hand as I looked at it and turned it over in my hand. I wondered if this was how Cedrick felt before he took his own life. Did he even bother to think of me, and if he did, was it love, or hate he felt. Probably hate, if he did have any thought of me, I can guarantee it was hate. That's the same way I felt about myself at the moment.

I looked at the screen, my lips touched Cedrick's cheek and he blushed. I couldn't help the tears that started falling again. I raised Jason's gun to my head. I looked at the screen, Cedrick's smile was on the screen. I closed my eyes, his smile would be the last moment of my life.

Bang!

$$$

Xtasy

Moan in my Mouth

The Final Chapter
One week later

-Cupid-

I woke up in the hospital. I looked around, everyone was crying as my eyes opened. On my right side were Nemo, Uncle Sam, and Shonda, Uncle Sam's wife. On my left side, Brianna stood with Tristian. My father was present, and my mother. I looked at everyone, they were all crying, staring at me with smiles.
"Good to have you back," my father was the first to speak. My mother kissed my forehead.
"I've been praying that you would come back to us. I always told you, prayer changes things." My mother said,
I couldn't talk, my mouth was dry, my tongue thick. I looked at Brianna, she was looking amazing, beyond beautiful. Tristan looked at me and smiled. "I'm happy you're doing okay. If something was to happen to you, I wouldn't have anyone to gamble with." Everyone laughed at him.
The door opened and a nurse and doctor walked in. "I'm sorry, family. I'm going to have to ask you all to exit the room so that I and my staff can run some tests on Mr. Patterson."
"Y'all heard the man, let's leave them be," my mother said as she kissed my forehead. "We'll come back later, baby. Okay." I nodded as I watched everyone file out of the room.
The last one to leave was Brianna. I tried to speak, but my mouth was too dry. Brianna kissed my lips. "Don't speak, it's okay. I forgive you. God gave you a second chance, don't waste it." Brianna smiled at me before she walked out.
A nurse helped me drink some lukewarm water from a straw. The water helped my throat so I could talk.
"Mr. Patterson, you're lucky to be alive." The doctor said as he looked through my file.
"What happened?" I asked.
"You don't remember anything?" He asked.

"I-I only remember," then it all came back to me. Amy, me, Cedrick. Cedrick caught us, me and Amy, having sex. He was there, I'm not sure why, but he was, and he caught us. He snatched me off of her, his fist pounded my face repeatedly. Then he hit me with something, a mic stand, no, a light stand. It knocked me unconscious.

"Cedrick, Amy," I muttered.

"Cedrick Montgomery. The sick bastard that beat you into a coma. He's dead, a gunshot wound to the head. Crazy bastard did it himself after he killed his own fiance."

"Cedrick's dead?" I said.

The doctor nodded. "Glad for it too."

"Amy, he-he killed her?"

"Sick bastard killed her, crazy thing, she was pregnant."

My heartbeat sped up. I lay my head back, I couldn't believe it. Cedrick killed Amy, then himself, and it was all my fault. I couldn't understand it. Why did I have to live, what did I have to gain? What was God trying to show me?

I thought back to the first day Cedrick moved back to Dallas. The smile he had on his face when he saw me, the moment he named me his best man. I betrayed him, my best friend. We grew up together, did everything together.

Amy, the smile she had on her face after we finished unloading their furniture. She was happy, ready to start a new chapter in her life, becoming Mrs. Amy Montgomery. I ruined it, I started it all, the domino effect.

That's why I can't understand why God let me live. What was the point, so, so I can relive the pain, the agony that I caused. It has to be more than that. But what?

Brianna walked to the window; she looked at me and smiled. Tristian stood beside her, he smiled. I forced a smile to my face, something I would have to get good at.

The doctor pumped some morphine into me. I lay my head back and thought about what I'd just been told. What was God trying to teach me? I knew having sex without being married was a sin. Lusting after women was as well. It was all I've ever done,

Moan in my Mouth

the only thing I've ever been good at. They say the end justifies the means. I prayed that it did. I didn't know what God had in store for me, I was just going to have to find out. I know one thing, chasing women was out of the equation. I planned on settling down with Brianna, that's if she would have me.

Then, as the medicine got stronger, I realized what God was trying to teach me. It is the quality of the burden we must learn from, not the weight. All my life I've been chasing women because I was too afraid to let one catch me. Countless nights, different women, and cold beers, the bachelor's life. Even a bachelor gets tired every now and then.

Sin starts in the mind, then it travels to the heart, the land where all of our treasures and wants are stored. I kept money and women there, but mainly, women. The devil knew it, so he fed me with all the women I could have, even my best friend's fiance. I ate it all up and got so full that I was bloated. I didn't even let the food digest before I refilled my plate. Damn devil's food!

The End!

Xtasy

About the Characters

Cupid - Cupid got discharged from the hospital. He paid for Cedrick's funeral, but he didn't attend, the pain was just too much to bear. Cupid sold Pandora Poison and started a new, improved film company. 'Cupid Chokehold'. Cupid put together a movie entitled, 'Pandora's Poison', which was a story about Amy, and Cedrick. The movie was #1 in the box office for four weeks straight and went on to make four hundred and fifty million dollars. Cupid now lives in New York with his wife Brianna, his stepson Tristian, and his newborn, little Ced'. Cupid continues to make motion pictures and 20% goes towards the non-profit organization he started, 'Crime of Passion'.

Belofante - Belofante went on to sell over ten million copies of his last album, which was the album Cedrick Montgomery produced. Belofante is no longer with Bloody Lyrics records, he's now under Def Jam. Belofante lived in Dallas Texas with his wife and two sons.

ZigZag - ZigZag went on to sell fifteen million copies of his debut album, "E is for Ethnicity." ZigZag bought himself out of his contract and is now signed to J. Cole's record label. He lives in Los Angeles as he continues to work on new music.

Franko Zay - Franko went on to break multiple records. His debut album, 'Barz behind Barz' made the number one in album sales and topped the charts for three weeks. Franko Zay went independent, and now has one of the hottest record labels in the industry, 'Foreign Nation'. Franko Zay lives in Atlanta with his sister and children.

Jason - Jason Woods had to file for bankruptcy due to all of his recording artists leaving the label. The bad publicity made protestors launch a campaign for owners to buy him out of his shares. Jason sold his shares and now lives with Brandi and their son in South Dallas.

Xtasy

Lock Down Publications and Ca$h Presents assisted publishing packages.

BASIC PACKAGE $499
Editing
Cover Design
Formatting

UPGRADED PACKAGE $800
Typing
Editing
Cover Design
Formatting

ADVANCE PACKAGE $1,200
Typing
Editing
Cover Design
Formatting
Copyright registration
Proofreading
Upload book to Amazon

LDP SUPREME PACKAGE $1,500
Typing
Editing
Cover Design
Formatting
Copyright registration
Proofreading
Set up Amazon account
Upload book to Amazon
Advertise on LDP Amazon and Facebook page

Moan in my Mouth

***Other services available upon request. Additional charges may apply
Lock Down Publications
P.O. Box 944
Stockbridge, GA 30281-9998
Phone # 470 303-9761

Xtasy

Submission Guideline

Submit the first three chapters of your completed manuscript to ldpsubmissions@gmail.com, subject line: Your book's title. The manuscript must be in a .doc file and sent as an attachment. Document should be in Times New Roman, double spaced and in size 12 font. Also, provide your synopsis and full contact information. If sending multiple submissions, they must each be in a separate email.

Have a story but no way to send it electronically? You can still submit to LDP/Ca$h Presents. Send in the first three chapters, written or typed, of your completed manuscript to:

LDP: Submissions Dept
Po Box 944
Stockbridge, Ga 30281

DO NOT send original manuscript. Must be a duplicate.

Provide your synopsis and a cover letter containing your full contact information.

Thanks for considering LDP and Ca$h Presents.

NEW RELEASES

LOYAL TO THE SOIL 3 by JIBRIL WILLIAMS
COKE BOYS by ROMELL TUKES
GRIMEY WAYS 2 by RAY VINCI
AN UNFORESEEN LOVE 3 by MEESHA
BORN IN THE GRAVE by SELF MADE TAY
MOAN IN MY MOUTH by XTASY

Xtasy

Coming Soon from Lock Down Publications/Ca$h Presents
BLOOD OF A BOSS **VI**
SHADOWS OF THE GAME II
TRAP BASTARD II
By **Askari**
LOYAL TO THE GAME **IV**
By **T.J. & Jelissa**
TRUE SAVAGE **VIII**
MIDNIGHT CARTEL IV
DOPE BOY MAGIC IV
CITY OF KINGZ III
NIGHTMARE ON SILENT AVE II
THE PLUG OF LIL MEXICO II
CLASSIC CITY II
By **Chris Green**
BLAST FOR ME **III**
A SAVAGE DOPEBOY III
CUTTHROAT MAFIA III
DUFFLE BAG CARTEL VII
HEARTLESS GOON VI
By **Ghost**
A HUSTLER'S DECEIT III
KILL ZONE II
BAE BELONGS TO ME III
TIL DEATH II
By **Aryanna**
KING OF THE TRAP III
By **T.J. Edwards**
GORILLAZ IN THE BAY V
3X KRAZY III

Moan in my Mouth

STRAIGHT BEAST MODE III
De'Kari
KINGPIN KILLAZ IV
STREET KINGS III
PAID IN BLOOD III
CARTEL KILLAZ IV
DOPE GODS III
Hood Rich
SINS OF A HUSTLA II
ASAD
RICH $AVAGE II
By Martell Troublesome Bolden
YAYO V
Bred In The Game 2
S. Allen
CREAM III
THE STREETS WILL TALK II
By Yolanda Moore
SON OF A DOPE FIEND III
HEAVEN GOT A GHETTO II
By Renta
LOYALTY AIN'T PROMISED III
By Keith Williams
I'M NOTHING WITHOUT HIS LOVE II
SINS OF A THUG II
TO THE THUG I LOVED BEFORE II
IN A HUSTLER I TRUST II
By Monet Dragun
QUIET MONEY IV
EXTENDED CLIP III

Xtasy

THUG LIFE IV
By **Trai'Quan**
THE STREETS MADE ME IV
By **Larry D. Wright**
IF YOU CROSS ME ONCE II
ANGEL IV
By **Anthony Fields**
THE STREETS WILL NEVER CLOSE IV
By K'ajji
HARD AND RUTHLESS III
KILLA KOUNTY III
By Khufu
MONEY GAME III
By Smoove Dolla
JACK BOYS VS DOPE BOYS II
A GANGSTA'S QUR'AN V
COKE GIRLZ II
COKE BOYS II
By Romell Tukes
MURDA WAS THE CASE II
Elijah R. Freeman
THE STREETS NEVER LET GO II
By Robert Baptiste
AN UNFORESEEN LOVE IV
By **Meesha**
KING OF THE TRENCHES III
by **GHOST & TRANAY ADAMS**

MONEY MAFIA II
By **Jibril Williams**
QUEEN OF THE ZOO III

Moan in my Mouth

By **Black Migo**
VICIOUS LOYALTY III
By **Kingpen**
A GANGSTA'S PAIN III
By **J-Blunt**
CONFESSIONS OF A JACKBOY III
By **Nicholas Lock**
GRIMEY WAYS III
By **Ray Vinci**
KING KILLA II
By **Vincent "Vitto" Holloway**
BETRAYAL OF A THUG II
By **Fre$h**
THE MURDER QUEENS II
By **Michael Gallon**
THE BIRTH OF A GANGSTER III
By **Delmont Player**
TREAL LOVE II
By **Le'Monica Jackson**
FOR THE LOVE OF BLOOD II
By **Jamel Mitchell**
RAN OFF ON DA PLUG II
By **Paper Boi Rari**
HOOD CONSIGLIERE II
By **Keese**
PRETTY GIRLS DO NASTY THINGS II
By **Nicole Goosby**
PROTÉGÉ OF A LEGEND II
By **Corey Robinson**
IT'S JUST ME AND YOU II

Xtasy
By Ah'Million
BORN IN THE GRAVE II
By Self Made Tay

Available Now

RESTRAINING ORDER **I & II**
By **CA$H & Coffee**
LOVE KNOWS NO BOUNDARIES **I II & III**
By **Coffee**
RAISED AS A GOON I, II, III & IV
BRED BY THE SLUMS I, II, III
BLAST FOR ME I & II
ROTTEN TO THE CORE I II III
A BRONX TALE I, II, III
DUFFLE BAG CARTEL I II III IV V VI
HEARTLESS GOON I II III IV V
A SAVAGE DOPEBOY I II
DRUG LORDS I II III
CUTTHROAT MAFIA I II
KING OF THE TRENCHES
By **Ghost**
LAY IT DOWN **I & II**
LAST OF A DYING BREED I II
BLOOD STAINS OF A SHOTTA I & II III
By **Jamaica**
LOYAL TO THE GAME I II III

Moan in my Mouth

LIFE OF SIN I, II III
By **TJ & Jelissa**
BLOODY COMMAS I & II
SKI MASK CARTEL I II & III
KING OF NEW YORK I II,III IV V
RISE TO POWER I II III
COKE KINGS I II III IV V
BORN HEARTLESS I II III IV
KING OF THE TRAP I II
By **T.J. Edwards**
IF LOVING HIM IS WRONG…I & II
LOVE ME EVEN WHEN IT HURTS I II III
By **Jelissa**
WHEN THE STREETS CLAP BACK I & II III
THE HEART OF A SAVAGE I II III IV
MONEY MAFIA
LOYAL TO THE SOIL I II III
By **Jibril Williams**
A DISTINGUISHED THUG STOLE MY HEART I II & III
LOVE SHOULDN'T HURT I II III IV
RENEGADE BOYS I II III IV
PAID IN KARMA I II III
SAVAGE STORMS I II III
AN UNFORESEEN LOVE I II III
By **Meesha**
A GANGSTER'S CODE I &, II III
A GANGSTER'S SYN I II III
THE SAVAGE LIFE I II III
CHAINED TO THE STREETS I II III
BLOOD ON THE MONEY I II III

Xtasy

A GANGSTA'S PAIN I II
By J-Blunt
PUSH IT TO THE LIMIT
By **Bre' Hayes**
BLOOD OF A BOSS **I, II, III, IV, V**
SHADOWS OF THE GAME
TRAP BASTARD
By **Askari**
THE STREETS BLEED MURDER **I, II & III**
THE HEART OF A GANGSTA I II& III
By **Jerry Jackson**
CUM FOR ME I II III IV V VI VII VIII
An **LDP Erotica Collaboration**
BRIDE OF A HUSTLA **I II & II**
THE FETTI GIRLS **I, II& III**
CORRUPTED BY A GANGSTA I, II III, IV
BLINDED BY HIS LOVE
THE PRICE YOU PAY FOR LOVE I, II ,III
DOPE GIRL MAGIC I II III
By **Destiny Skai**
WHEN A GOOD GIRL GOES BAD
By **Adrienne**
THE COST OF LOYALTY I II III
By Kweli
A GANGSTER'S REVENGE **I II III & IV**
THE BOSS MAN'S DAUGHTERS I II III IV V
A SAVAGE LOVE **I & II**
BAE BELONGS TO ME I II
A HUSTLER'S DECEIT I, II, III
WHAT BAD BITCHES DO I, II, III

Moan in my Mouth

SOUL OF A MONSTER I II III
KILL ZONE
A DOPE BOY'S QUEEN I II III
TIL DEATH
By **Aryanna**
A KINGPIN'S AMBITON
A KINGPIN'S AMBITION **II**
I MURDER FOR THE DOUGH
By **Ambitious**
TRUE SAVAGE I II III IV V VI VII
DOPE BOY MAGIC I, II, III
MIDNIGHT CARTEL I II III
CITY OF KINGZ I II
NIGHTMARE ON SILENT AVE
THE PLUG OF LIL MEXICO II
CLASSIC CITY
By **Chris Green**
A DOPEBOY'S PRAYER
By **Eddie "Wolf" Lee**
THE KING CARTEL **I, II & III**
By **Frank Gresham**
THESE NIGGAS AIN'T LOYAL **I, II & III**
By **Nikki Tee**
GANGSTA SHYT **I II &III**
By **CATO**
THE ULTIMATE BETRAYAL
By **Phoenix**
BOSS'N UP **I , II & III**
By **Royal Nicole**
I LOVE YOU TO DEATH

Xtasy

By **Destiny J**
I RIDE FOR MY HITTA
I STILL RIDE FOR MY HITTA
By **Misty Holt**
LOVE & CHASIN' PAPER
By **Qay Crockett**
TO DIE IN VAIN
SINS OF A HUSTLA
By **ASAD**
BROOKLYN HUSTLAZ
By **Boogsy Morina**
BROOKLYN ON LOCK I & II
By **Sonovia**
GANGSTA CITY
By **Teddy Duke**
A DRUG KING AND HIS DIAMOND I & II III
A DOPEMAN'S RICHES
HER MAN, MINE'S TOO I, II
CASH MONEY HO'S
THE WIFEY I USED TO BE I II
PRETTY GIRLS DO NASTY THINGS
By Nicole Goosby
TRAPHOUSE KING **I II & III**
KINGPIN KILLAZ I II III
STREET KINGS I II
PAID IN BLOOD **I II**
CARTEL KILLAZ I II III
DOPE GODS I II
By **Hood Rich**
LIPSTICK KILLAH **I, II, III**

Moan in my Mouth

CRIME OF PASSION I II & III
FRIEND OR FOE I II III
By **Mimi**
STEADY MOBBN' **I, II, III**
THE STREETS STAINED MY SOUL I II III
By **Marcellus Allen**
WHO SHOT YA **I, II, III**
SON OF A DOPE FIEND I II
HEAVEN GOT A GHETTO
Renta
GORILLAZ IN THE BAY **I II III IV**
TEARS OF A GANGSTA I II
3X KRAZY I II
STRAIGHT BEAST MODE I II
DE'KARI
TRIGGADALE I II III
MURDAROBER WAS THE CASE
Elijah R. Freeman
GOD BLESS THE TRAPPERS I, II, III
THESE SCANDALOUS STREETS I, II, III
FEAR MY GANGSTA I, II, III IV, V
THESE STREETS DON'T LOVE NOBODY I, II
BURY ME A G I, II, III, IV, V
A GANGSTA'S EMPIRE I, II, III, IV
THE DOPEMAN'S BODYGAURD I II
THE REALEST KILLAZ I II III
THE LAST OF THE OGS I II III
Tranay Adams
THE STREETS ARE CALLING
Duquie Wilson

Xtasy

MARRIED TO A BOSS I II III
By Destiny Skai & Chris Green
KINGZ OF THE GAME I II III IV V VI
Playa Ray
SLAUGHTER GANG I II III
RUTHLESS HEART I II III
By Willie Slaughter
FUK SHYT
By Blakk Diamond
DON'T F#CK WITH MY HEART I II
By Linnea
ADDICTED TO THE DRAMA I II III
IN THE ARM OF HIS BOSS II
By Jamila
YAYO I II III IV
A SHOOTER'S AMBITION I II
BRED IN THE GAME
By S. Allen
TRAP GOD I II III
RICH $AVAGE
MONEY IN THE GRAVE I II III
By Martell Troublesome Bolden
FOREVER GANGSTA
GLOCKS ON SATIN SHEETS I II
By Adrian Dulan
TOE TAGZ I II III IV
LEVELS TO THIS SHYT I II
IT'S JUST ME AND YOU
By Ah'Million
KINGPIN DREAMS I II III

Moan in my Mouth

RAN OFF ON DA PLUG
By Paper Boi Rari
CONFESSIONS OF A GANGSTA I II III IV
CONFESSIONS OF A JACKBOY I II
By Nicholas Lock
I'M NOTHING WITHOUT HIS LOVE
SINS OF A THUG
TO THE THUG I LOVED BEFORE
A GANGSTA SAVED XMAS
IN A HUSTLER I TRUST
By Monet Dragun
CAUGHT UP IN THE LIFE I II III
THE STREETS NEVER LET GO
By Robert Baptiste
NEW TO THE GAME I II III
MONEY, MURDER & MEMORIES I II III
By **Malik D. Rice**
LIFE OF A SAVAGE I II III
A GANGSTA'S QUR'AN I II III IV
MURDA SEASON I II III
GANGLAND CARTEL I II III
CHI'RAQ GANGSTAS I II III
KILLERS ON ELM STREET I II III
JACK BOYZ N DA BRONX I II III
A DOPEBOY'S DREAM I II III
JACK BOYS VS DOPE BOYS
COKE GIRLZ
COKE BOYS
By Romell Tukes
LOYALTY AIN'T PROMISED I II

Xtasy

By Keith Williams
QUIET MONEY I II III
THUG LIFE I II III
EXTENDED CLIP I II
By **Trai'Quan**
THE STREETS MADE ME I II III
By **Larry D. Wright**
THE ULTIMATE SACRIFICE I, II, III, IV, V, VI
KHADIFI
IF YOU CROSS ME ONCE
ANGEL I II III
IN THE BLINK OF AN EYE
By **Anthony Fields**
THE LIFE OF A HOOD STAR
By Ca$h & Rashia Wilson
THE STREETS WILL NEVER CLOSE I II III
By **K'ajji**
CREAM I II
THE STREETS WILL TALK
By Yolanda Moore
NIGHTMARES OF A HUSTLA I II III
By King Dream
CONCRETE KILLA I II III
VICIOUS LOYALTY I II
By Kingpen
HARD AND RUTHLESS I II
MOB TOWN 251
THE BILLIONAIRE BENTLEYS I II III
By Von Diesel
GHOST MOB

Moan in my Mouth

Stilloan Robinson
MOB TIES I II III IV V VI
By SayNoMore
BODYMORE MURDERLAND I II III
THE BIRTH OF A GANGSTER I II
By Delmont Player
FOR THE LOVE OF A BOSS
By C. D. Blue
MOBBED UP I II III IV
THE BRICK MAN I II III IV
THE COCAINE PRINCESS I II III IV V
By King Rio
KILLA KOUNTY I II III
By Khufu
MONEY GAME I II
By Smoove Dolla
A GANGSTA'S KARMA I II
By FLAME
KING OF THE TRENCHES I II
by **GHOST & TRANAY ADAMS**
QUEEN OF THE ZOO I II
By **Black Migo**
GRIMEY WAYS I II
By Ray Vinci
XMAS WITH AN ATL SHOOTER
By Ca$h & Destiny Skai
KING KILLA
By Vincent "Vitto" Holloway
BETRAYAL OF A THUG
By Fre$h

Xtasy

THE MURDER QUEENS
By Michael Gallon
TREAL LOVE
By Le'Monica Jackson
FOR THE LOVE OF BLOOD
By Jamel Mitchell
HOOD CONSIGLIERE
By Keese
PROTÉGÉ OF A LEGEND
By Corey Robinson
BORN IN THE GRAVE
By Self Made Tay
MOAN IN MY MOUTH
By XTASY

Moan in my Mouth

BOOKS BY LDP'S CEO, CA$H

TRUST IN NO MAN
TRUST IN NO MAN 2
TRUST IN NO MAN 3
BONDED BY BLOOD
SHORTY GOT A THUG
THUGS CRY
THUGS CRY 2
THUGS CRY 3
TRUST NO BITCH
TRUST NO BITCH 2
TRUST NO BITCH 3
TIL MY CASKET DROPS
RESTRAINING ORDER
RESTRAINING ORDER 2
IN LOVE WITH A CONVICT
LIFE OF A HOOD STAR
XMAS WITH AN ATL SHOOTER

Xtasy

CPSIA information can be obtained
at www.ICGtesting.com
Printed in the USA
LVHW081100290822
727089LV00007B/106